Boy, they like this in Los Angeles.

From the top of his cowboy hat to the tips of his leather boots, he was one tall, gorgeous hunk of man.

Julie flashed him her best smile and tried to focus on what he was saying. "You could help me with what?"

She liked the way he squirmed just a little as she studied him. Handsome as he was, he didn't strike her as the kind of guy who'd be bashful around women. She also liked the muscles that showed through his white T-shirt. Brawn like his was the result of hard outdoor work and not a gym.

He took off his hat and ran a hand through his cropped dark chocolate-brown hair. "Handling the sander, ma'am."

Was it possible he was just being neighborly and not flirting?

She hoped not....

Dear Reader,

We've been busy here at Silhouette Romance cooking up the next batch of tender, emotion-filled romances to add extra sizzle to your day.

First on the menu is Laurey Bright's modern-day Sleeping Beauty story, *With His Kiss* (#1660). Next, Melissa McClone whips up a sensuous, *Survivor*-like tale when total opposites must survive two weeks on an island, in *The Wedding Adventure* (#1661). Then bite into the next juicy SOULMATES series addition, *The Knight's Kiss* (#1663) by Nicole Burnham, about a cursed knight and the modern-day princess who has the power to unlock his hardened heart.

We hope you have room for more, because we have three other treats in store for you. First, popular Silhouette Romance author Susan Meier turns on the heat in *The Nanny Solution* (#1662), the third in her DAYCARE DADS miniseries about single fathers who learn the ABCs of love. Then, in Jill Limber's *Captivating a Cowboy* (#1664), are a city girl and a dyed-in-the-wool cowboy a recipe for disaster…or romance? Finally, Lissa Manley dishes out the laughs with *The Bachelor Chronicles* (#1665), in which a sassy journalist is assigned to get the city's most eligible—and stubborn—bachelor to go on a blind date!

I guarantee these heartwarming stories will keep you satisfied until next month when we serve up our list of great summer reads.

Happy reading!

Mary-Theresa Hussey

Mary-Theresa Hussey
Senior Editor

Please address questions and book requests to:
Silhouette Reader Service
U.S.: 3010 Walden Ave., P.O. Box 1325, Buffalo, NY 14269
Canadian: P.O. Box 609, Fort Erie, Ont. L2A 5X3

Captivating a Cowboy

JILL LIMBER

SILHOUETTE *Romance*®

Published by Silhouette Books

America's Publisher of Contemporary Romance

To Kathy—best buddy and cosmic sister. This one's for you!

Acknowledgments:
Many thanks to James Weippert—for letting me pick his brain
and for his service to his country as a Navy SEAL.
Thanks to Dr. Dick O'Connor and Dr. Ernie Tucker
for all things medical, along with friendship.
Special thanks to Bryn Willson for her wonderful poetry.

 SILHOUETTE BOOKS

ISBN 0-373-19664-4

CAPTIVATING A COWBOY

Books by Jill Limber

Silhouette Romance

The 15 lb. Matchmaker #1593
Captivating a Cowboy #1664

JILL LIMBER

lives in San Diego with her husband. Now that her children are grown, their two dogs keep her company while she sits at her computer writing stories. A native Californian, she enjoys the beach, loves to swim in the ocean, and for relaxation she daydreams and reads romances. You can learn more about Jill by visiting her Web site at http://www.JillLimber.com.

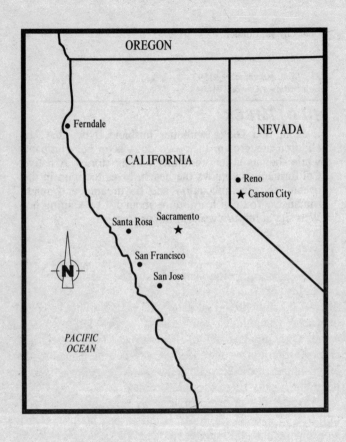

Chapter One

Tony saw her the instant she walked into the hardware store. He paused in the aisle and studied the fine piece of eye candy that had sauntered in off the street, putting every fiber of his male being on alert. Her long ponytail twitched over bared shoulders. Snug shorts dipped below a slim waist, showing a band of firm brown flesh where her cropped top didn't quite meet up with denim. Long slender legs completed the sexy little female package he judged to be about twenty-five years old.

Conversations dropped off one by one until every man in the store, including old Mr. Dunn, turned his head. Cliff, working behind the counter, looked like a deer caught in headlights as she approached him.

Tony was too far away to hear what she asked, but he could see the tips of Cliff's ears turn a bright red. He pointed to the back of the store. She turned, and Tony felt like someone had sucked all the oxygen out of the place. She had a face like an angel, with big blue-green eyes and a generous upper lip over a full lower lip. A mouth made for kissing and a body built straight out of every man's fantasy.

Suddenly the fact that every guy in the store was probably thinking the same thing annoyed the hell out of him. He had a sudden irrational and possessively childish urge to tell them he had seen her first.

He shook his head at his own foolishness. He had better things to do with his time than stand in Nilsen's Hardware and have fantasies that could get him arrested in half the states in the country. If he was going to get his house finished on his land before the cold weather set in so he could move out of his tiny unheated trailer, he needed to get going.

Yeah, right, he thought, rooted to the spot as he watched the utterly female way she walked.

She made her way to the power tools and bent over the boxes that contained sanders. Tony bit back a groan and headed for the counter to pay for his supplies.

A man could only take so much.

Cliff rang up the sack of nails and caulking. He made change, his attention not on what he was doing. Tony had to grab the coins before they dropped on the counter.

"Who is she?" Tony asked, resisting the urge to turn around and take another long look.

Cliff shrugged and leaned to the side so he could see around Tony. "Don't know. This is the first she's been in here."

She had to be new in town, Tony thought. In Ferndale strangers never went unnoticed. Especially women who looked as good as this one.

He lingered until Cliff straightened up and smoothed a hand down the front of his shirt, alerting Tony to the fact she was on her way to the counter. He moved a few feet away to look at a display of saw blades.

She walked by him carrying a box and trailing the fragrance of summer flowers, sweet and fresh.

"Does this sander come with instructions?" She laid a credit card beside the box.

Tony stifled a groan. He was all for equal opportunity, but unskilled women and power tools were generally a bad combination.

Cliff slid her plastic credit card across the counter, swiped it through his machine and handed it back before Tony could read the name on it.

Cliff mumbled and reached to open the box. He waved a piece of paper. "Sorry, miss, no operating instructions. Just the usual safety warnings." He handed her the credit slip to sign.

Unable to help himself, Tony stepped closer, hoping his carnal thoughts didn't show on his face. "Excuse me, miss. Maybe I could help."

Julie turned to glance at the great-looking man she had noticed lurking by a display of big metal wheels with wicked teeth. Boy, they sure didn't grow them like this in Los Angeles. From the top of his cowboy hat to the tips of his leather boots, he was one tall gorgeous hunk of man.

She flashed him her best smile. "Could help me with what?" she asked, wondering exactly what he meant.

She liked the way he squirmed just a little as she studied him. Shy, perhaps. Handsome as he was, he didn't strike her as the kind of guy who would be bashful around women. She also liked the muscles that showed through the close fit of his white T-shirt. Brawn like his was the result of hard outdoor work and not a gym.

He took off his hat and ran a big square hand through his cropped dark chocolate-brown hair, then gestured to the box the middle-aged clerk struggled to repackage. "The sander, ma'am."

The cowboy was blushing. She swallowed a smile. Was it possible he was just being neighborly and not flirting?

She hoped not.

She was going to be in Ferndale all summer, and had no friends here. No one she knew from Los Angeles was likely to come for a visit. She'd been dreading being stuck in this small town for three long months.

Quaint Victorian Ferndale hadn't changed any since she'd left almost ten years ago to go to college. Now that she'd used her credit card, within hours everyone in town would know she was back in Northern California. Give her a big city any day. There was no such thing as privacy in a small town.

She winked at him. "Thanks, cowboy, but I think I can manage."

At least she could learn. With her budget and time limit, she had to become adept quickly to finish all the things that needed doing to her grandmother's house.

Her house now.

She wanted get the place fixed up and put it on the market. She had to get back to L.A. before the school year started.

He tapped his forefinger on the box. "Do you have any experience with power tools?"

The cowboy had a polite earnestness about him she found appealing. The men she knew were so into their own image and being cool they would never show the kind of interest she saw on his handsome face.

She shrugged, amused that he would assume she couldn't manage by herself because she was a woman. She was smart and could figure out how to do what needed to be done.

Julie glanced around at the men who had gathered to listen openly to their conversation, then gave them a smile.

"How hard can it be? You all know how to use them,

don't you?'' she asked sweetly, then picked up the box and
sauntered out onto Main Street.

Every pair of eyes watched her leave. As she disappeared
from sight, Tony swore he heard a collective male sigh
from inside the store.

Tony turned to Cliff. ''Who is she?''

Cliff scratched his bald head, still staring at the now
empty door. ''Dunno.''

Tony reached over and pulled the credit slip out of
Cliff's fingers.

''Julie Kerns.'' He read aloud.

''That was little Julie Kerns?'' Mr. Dunn peered around
Tony trying to see the slip of paper.

Tony turned to stare at the old man. ''You know her?''

Mr. Dunn nodded. ''She used to live here. Moved in with
her grandma when she was a little girl after her folks died.''

''Where does her grandmother live?''

''Doesn't. Her grandma was Bessie Morgan. Died about
two months ago.''

Tony thought for a minute. The name was vaguely familiar. ''The blue-and-white Queen Anne style house with
the vines over by the church?''

Mr. Dunn nodded. ''Yup. Heard Julie got the house.
Must be moving in.''

Tony stored that bit of information away and left the
store whistling.

He'd find a reason to go and pay the little lady a call
and remind her how neighborly Ferndale could be.

Tony stood on the sidewalk in the hot noon sun and
shifted the ladder on his shoulder to a more comfortable
position. He contemplated the cottage belonging to the very
enticing Julie Kerns.

Two things came to mind.

First, the house was a marvel of workmanship, with all the trim and special touches that went into a Queen Anne. Not as fussy as most Victorians, he'd always liked the design.

Second, the place needed a heck of a lot of work.

For starters, the top two wooden steps to the porch were rotten. He glanced up and noted the rain gutter had rusted through in several places. That explained the rot.

He leaned the new ladder she'd ordered against the side of his truck and hefted the five gallon cans of plastering compound and primer.

Skirting the rotten wood, he climbed the stairs and set the cans beside the front door. The doorbell, a round crank set in the wall, rang loud enough to be heard in the next block.

Within moments, he saw her through the beveled glass window set in the middle of the door. She wore baggy old jeans and a big shirt. He missed yesterday's outfit.

Julie opened the door and raised an eyebrow. "Hello, cowboy."

He grinned at her and tipped his hat. "Afternoon, Miss Kerns." He'd forgotten how pretty she was.

"Please, it's Julie." She didn't seem surprised that he knew her name.

"I'm Tony. Tony Graham."

She gave him that great smile of hers, then glanced down and spotted the cans. "Do you work at the hardware store?"

"No, ma'am. Just doing Cliff a favor. His wife took the truck to Redding to do some shopping."

Tony hoisted the cans and she stood aside so he could enter. "Where do you want these?"

"Upstairs. But you can leave them right there."

"I'll take them up for you. Lead the way."

He enjoyed the sway of her hips as she climbed the stairs ahead of him.

She turned into one of the front bedrooms. He set the cans inside the door. She'd been busy. All the furniture had been pushed into the middle of the room and covered with a tarp.

Tony gave a low whistle when he looked up and saw the water damage to the ceiling and walls. Big chunks of plaster were missing. "Roof?"

She nodded. "Yes. Bessie hated to spend money and waited until the leak got really bad before she had it repaired."

He nodded. Lots of people put off work, then ended up paying more. He didn't understand their logic.

Dubious that a novice had a chance of doing a decent plaster job, Tony wandered over to a damaged wall and turned to eye the book she held. "You ever do any plaster repair?"

"Not yet." She slapped the book she was holding closed and set it on top of the tarp, then put her hands on her hips.

She sure did look determined.

She studied him for so long he wanted to squirm. Then she squared her shoulder as if she had made a decision and asked, "Have you had lunch?"

It took him a moment to react. He didn't expect the question. "No. I was just about to take a break." His lunch was in his truck.

"Good. Have lunch with me."

Tony was both surprised and pleased at her invitation. He had been trying to decide how to ask her out. Now they could get acquainted over a sandwich at the kitchen table.

"Sure. That would be great."

"I have to warn you, I have an ulterior motive."

Tony raised an eyebrow as a quick fantasy shot through his mind.

She tapped her book with a slender forefinger. "I want to pick your brain about plastering techniques."

Oh, well, he thought, feeling a little deflated, at least she wanted to have lunch with him.

He followed her downstairs and instead of turning toward the back of the house where he assumed the kitchen would be, she went out the front door.

"We're going out?"

Julie looked back at him over her shoulder with a smile. "My treat. I don't cook."

He wanted to ask her why not. Cooking was basic for existing as far as he was concerned. Did she eat all her meals out? It seemed a little too soon to ask. Some women got so prickly when a guy asked questions like that.

"Okay." He wasn't comfortable with her picking up the tab even if it was her idea, but they could discuss that when the time came.

Tony closed the front door behind him and walked with her a half block until they hit Main Street. They chatted about how the town had not changed at all in the years since she had left.

"Village Bakery okay with you?"

"Sure." He'd eat the lunch in his truck for supper.

They found a table and gave the waitress their order.

Julie smiled at him and he went warm all over. What a beauty, with her streaked brown hair and blue-green eyes. He smiled back and noticed she had flecks of gold in her eyes that matched the streaks in her hair.

"Now, about plastering."

He didn't care why she had invited him to lunch. If she smiled at him like that she could have anything she wanted. "What do you need to know?"

She shrugged. "Everything."

Tony laughed loudly enough that everyone in the bakery turned to look at the two of them.

"You sure you want to do this yourself? I'd be glad to help." He could take some time off from building his house.

She hesitated for a moment, glancing down at the table, then back up at him. "No, thanks. I'm going to do it myself, but I'm not above wangling a few tips. How did you learn to do plastering?"

"My dad and I built the house my folks live in now when I was a teenager. He was in construction before he started ranching."

"Do your parents live around here?"

"No. Wyoming."

"How did you come to live in Ferndale?"

He felt a quick stab of the familiar pain associated with the accident, Jimmy's death, and how he had come to be where he was. "I inherited a piece of property just outside of town. I'm building my own place there now."

The waitress set their sandwiches in front of them. He thanked her and between bites, steered the conversation back to plastering. He told Julie everything he could think of that would help her do the job.

She asked a few questions, then mentioned her grandmother again, commenting on all the stuff she still needed to clean out.

He eyed her curiously. "You called your grandmother by her first name?"

Her expressive blue-green eyes became shuttered for a moment, then she gave him a rueful smile. "Bessie never liked being called Grandma."

Tony tucked that bit of information away to ponder later.

"You have a lot of work to do on the place before you move in." He hadn't missed the peeling wallpaper and chipped paint.

She laughed. "I'm *moved* in, but it's temporary. As soon

as I can get the placed fixed up, it goes on the market and I go home.''

''Where's home?'' He didn't like the thought of her leaving Ferndale. He had plans to get to know her better.

A *lot* better.

''Los Angeles.''

He couldn't think of a worse place to live. ''Why?''

She raised a finely arched eyebrow. ''Why what?''

''Why do you live there?'' It must be for her job.

She laughed. ''Because I like it. Why do you live in Ferndale?''

He grinned at her. ''Because I like it.'' Or at least he would when he could move into his own home.

''What do you do in L.A.?'' He wondered what kind of job would keep her there.

''I teach high school. English.''

The waitress brought the bill and they both reached for it. ''I invited you.'' Julie jerked the slip of paper out of his hand.

''Half?'' He didn't let women buy him meals. It might be old-fashioned, but it didn't set right.

''No. Then I'll feel guilty for picking your brain the whole time we ate.''

Tony shrugged, then thought of a plan. ''Okay. But only if you agree to have dinner with me tomorrow night.''

Julie watched him for a minute. He sensed her hesitation, then she gave him another of her great smiles. ''Deal.''

He watched her walk up to the counter to pay.

He'd never had a teacher who looked like Ms. Kerns. The boys in her classes probably had a hard time keeping their minds on the subject matter when she was standing in front of the class.

He stood up and pulled two bills out of his pocket for the tip. She saw him leave the money on the table and rolled her eyes.

They walked back to her house in companionable silence.

He glanced over at her. She could teach anywhere. Why would she choose to live in a big smelly city like Los Angeles? Maybe a guy kept her there. He didn't like the thought.

"So you teach English. Fond of the classics?" He liked her hair. So many different shades of brown.

She shrugged. "I'm fond of all kinds of books."

He had been, too, once. He had devoured books, losing himself for hours in them. Since the accident he had to struggle to read, and the frustration ruined the pleasure.

When they got to her place Tony unloaded the rest of her order and carried a ladder and bag of small hand tools upstairs. The banister was loose and needed bracing.

He found Julie leaning against a piece of covered furniture, holding her how-to book and frowning.

"You need me to stay?" He glanced over at the book she studied. Doing plaster work took some skill. Even with everything he'd told her he was skeptical that she could manage alone.

"Nope." She glanced up from the page she studied and smiled. "Remember? I'm going to do it myself."

He wondered why she was so stubborn about not having help. He'd be willing to take time off from working on his own house. He didn't say anything. From the set of her shoulders and the jut of her chin it was obvious she was intent on tackling the job herself.

He'd give her the rest of the day to see how hard the job was, then come back and see if she'd changed her mind about his help.

He reached into the bag and pulled out the goggles and dust mask he had purchased and added to her order.

"Come over here." Tony motioned to her.

When she hesitated, he said, "Just more friendly advice."

She shrugged and moved to his side. Her hair smelled like lemons, and he fought the urge to lean closer and inhale.

He positioned her under the worst of the damage, liking the feel of her warm skin under her cotton shirt.

Reluctantly he let go of her and pointed to the ceiling. "Always wear these." He held up the mask and goggles. "They'll get in your way, but you'll get used to them. Be sure to chip off all the stained plaster. Otherwise, the stain will bleed through your new paint."

"Okay." She glanced up to the ceiling and back to his face.

Tony handed over the safety equipment and wanted to reach for her, the urge to kiss her strong.

He pulled back. Whoa, way too soon for a move like that, he thought. Instead he stepped away and opened the ladder, positioning it under a gaping hole in the ceiling. "Good luck."

As he turned to leave, she said, "'Bye, Tony. And thanks."

"Anytime. Thanks for lunch." He gave her a smile before he started down the stairs.

Julie watched him go, then glanced down at the goggles and mask dangling from her fingers. His concern about her safety touched her.

She ran a finger over the ridges in the blue mask. The handsome man had some kind of problem with speech comprehension and she couldn't quite put her finger on it. She'd noticed how he'd watched her face intently as she spoke, and then there would be a bit of lag time before he replied. She didn't think he was deaf, but perhaps she was wrong and he was reading lips.

Curiosity got the better of her and she went out to the

upstairs landing and leaned over the rail just as he opened the front door.

"Tony?" She kept her voice very quiet.

He turned immediately. "Yes?"

Well, his hearing was fine. She groped for something to say. "Ah, if you see Cliff, tell him thanks for the delivery."

He tipped his hat. "Sure thing. Be careful not to lean on that banister. It's loose." He closed the door behind him.

She knew the railing was loose. She just hadn't gotten to that chapter in her fix-it book yet.

She glanced around the upstairs landing. How hard could it be? She had the tools and the how-to book. If she sold the place as a fixer-upper she would get a lot less for it, and she needed the money.

Her dream was to take time off teaching to write. She had ideas for several children's books, but she needed the time. Teaching seemed to drain away her creativity.

She'd sublet her apartment at the beach for the summer and planned to spend her vacation repairing plaster and painting. Then she'd put the house up for sale and go back to Los Angeles in time to start teaching. When the house sold, she'd take a leave of absence to write.

Julie walked back into the bedroom. She'd checked recent sale prices of Victorians in Ferndale. She figured she could take next year, maybe even the next two, off if she moved away from the beach and into a cheaper apartment.

There were a few pieces of her grandmother's furniture she'd like to keep, but the rest she could offer with the house. She made a mental note to talk to the people who ran the Foggy Bottom Antiques Store and Cream City Antiques. They might be willing to take some of it on consignment.

Her mind wandered back to Tony. Why had she agreed to dinner tomorrow night? She didn't plan to get involved. She'd ended her on-again-off-again relationship with Alan before she left L.A. He had indicated he wanted to get more serious, and she wasn't interested in a commitment.

Julie rummaged through the bag from the hardware store and laid out the tools recommended in the book. In L.A. she wouldn't think of going out with someone she didn't know. But here in Ferndale nobody was really a stranger.

She turned her attention back to work and did a quick scan of the section on repairing plaster. She climbed the ladder to get to the damaged wall, then donned the mask and goggles. Within minutes of chipping away at the plaster dust covered her hair and sifted into her bra.

She sneezed and a cloud of fine white powder drifted down.

Why would anyone choose to do this kind of work? She thought of Tony as she wiped at her face with her sleeve, then climbed back down the ladder to tuck a rag in the waistband of her jeans.

She flipped on the portable compact disk player and with Jimmy Buffett wailing about cheeseburgers in paradise, she went back to work.

By midafternoon her arms ached. Even though she had worn the goggles, she had to use saline drops to get the dust out of her eyes. But she'd made good progress. All the old plaster was down. Tomorrow she would start patching. Her arms were too sore to start today.

Julie took a shower and washed the plaster out of her hair. Then she fixed herself a snack and contemplated what she would do with the rest of the afternoon.

The closets. Bessie had a lifetime of stuff stored on the shelves and in the cupboards. Julie felt like an intruder going through her grandmother's belongings, but it had to be done.

The woman had never shared anything personal with Julie, and would probably be horrified that someone was poking through her things, but Julie couldn't get rid of them without sorting them.

Reluctantly she trudged back up the stairs and started in the room where she had slept as a teenager.

She slipped off her shoes and used the chair from the dressing table to reach the shelves in the closet. There were boxes of hats and gloves that must have dated back to the forties. Bessie had worn a hat to church every Sunday.

Julie wondered if they would be worth anything at a vintage clothing store. She knew of a good one in L.A. she could call, she thought as she piled them in a corner of the room.

After she finished the closet, she opened the cupboards above the closet. Large boxes marked Bedding were stacked to the top of the space. Had her grandmother saved old bedding as well as old clothes?

Julie reached as high as she could and tugged at the top box. It seemed to be caught on the box below. She should go get the ladder, but she was tired and the thought of getting down to get the darned thing was too much work.

She gave the box a yank and it slid toward her. The cardboard came apart in her hands and a waterfall of huge leather-bound books tumbled down on her, knocking her from the chair.

As she hit the floor beside the bed she heard a sound that reminded her of a dry twig breaking.

She lay up against the bed, stunned. The books were ledgers from the insurance business her grandfather had run in Ferndale for years.

Furious with herself for being so stupid, she struggled to sit up. It hurt to move her right arm and she had a gash on the inside of her left elbow that was starting to bleed freely. Her legs felt okay, so she struggled to her feet and grabbed a towel from the bathroom to hold against the cut.

She got as far as the top of the stairs when she started

to feel dizzy, so she lowered herself to the top step and leaned against the wall. She needed a moment to think about what she'd do next.

Tony skirted the rotten boards on Julie's steps and paused at the front door. He glanced down at the plaster finishing tool he held in his hand. His offer of help so soon after she had turned him down twice might make her mad, but getting a smooth finish to match the rest of the room was tricky, and he wanted to help her out.

He turned the crank on the old doorbell.

"Come in."

He heard her faintly through the heavy door. He stepped into the dim foyer and glanced up the stairs to find her sitting on the top step. She'd washed her hair and changed clothes.

He smiled. "Wear yourself out?"

"Something like that," she said, her voice flat and low.

She was mad at him and he hadn't even offered his help yet. She'd undoubtedly spotted the trowel in his hand.

But then he realized as he looked up at her something was wrong. She was leaning against the wall as if she needed the support. Her face was pale and drawn.

He dropped the trowel and took the stairs two at a time, flipped on the light switch and crouched down on the step below her.

"You showed up at just the right time," she said, an edge of pain in her voice.

He could see her struggle not to cry and it tore him up inside. "What happened?" He didn't want to touch her until she told him where she hurt.

"I was cleaning out a cupboard and pulled a box of books down on my head."

"Did you fall?" He cupped her face gently in his palms and studied the bruise blooming on her cheek.

"Yes," she said with a catch in her voice.

He dropped his hands from her face. "Off the ladder?"

She shook her head. "I was standing on a chair."

"Did you black out?" This was not the time to tell her how foolish she had been. Besides he could tell by her voice she had already told herself the same thing.

"No. I remember every last detail." She attempted a laugh but it came out as a little sob.

Tony didn't want her to fall apart so he patted her briskly on the knee and said, "You're doing fine."

Julie nodded and seemed to pull herself together.

"Tell me what else hurts besides your cheek."

"It hurts when I move my arm."

She had a dark green towel in her lap. She'd been cradling her right arm with her left hand. "Okay. What part of your arm?"

"My shoulder."

She had on an oversize blue shirt. "I need to unbutton your blouse, okay?"

She gave him a lopsided smile. "Is that the best line you have, cowboy?" she asked with a little hitch in her voice.

He returned the smile, relieved she still had her sassy sense of humor. "It'll have to do for now."

He unbuttoned her shirt and gently eased the fabric off her shoulder, trying to ignore the electric-blue lacy bra strap.

He ran his fingers lightly along her clavicle, stopping at a big lumpy spot. There was no doubt the bone was fractured. Swelling and discoloration had already begun.

Carefully he pulled the shirt back in place and buttoned her up. "You broke your collarbone."

"I was afraid of that. I heard a snapping sound when I hit the floor."

"What else?"

"I have a cut on my elbow. I think I landed on the corner of the bed frame." She glanced down at her left arm.

He needed some space. She was leaning with her left arm against the wall. "I'm going to help you up and we're going down into the kitchen so I can get a good look at your arm."

"Okay."

"Can you walk?" He couldn't carry her without hurting her and he needed to assess her overall condition.

Her chin came up. "Yes."

He stood up and backed down a step to give her the room to stand. She braced herself against the wall and swayed a bit.

"Dizzy?' He grabbed her hips to steady her, braced to catch her if she fainted.

"A little."

There was no color in her face and her skin looked clammy.

"I'm going to get beside you." Tony stepped up to the same stair she was on and reached under the back of her shirt, grasping a handful of the waistband of her pants.

"Just take it slow."

She nodded and started down the steep stairs, wincing as each step jarred her arm.

He guided her to a kitchen chair and she lowered herself gingerly. He knelt on the floor beside her and pulled the towel away from her arm. A jagged gash about three inches long lay across the elbow joint along the inside of her arm. The towel was so dark he hadn't noticed the blood.

He went blank for a moment and then pulled himself together. On missions he'd acted purely on his training. It was different with Julie. She shook him up.

Tony pulled himself together and said, "It's still bleeding. I need to put some pressure on it. Where are the clean towels?"

"The drawer next to the sink."

He found a stack of white dish towels and made a thick pad with one, pressed it against the cut, then wrapped it tightly with a second towel.

He slid into the chair next to her. "Okay, that should hold you until we can get it stitched up."

She raised an eyebrow and gave him a long look. "You want to do it? My grandmother's sewing box is in the living room."

He shook his head, knowing she was kidding. He had put stitches in before, but that was when there were no medics around. Her beautiful smooth skin deserved more of an expert than he was.

She stared at him. "Where did you learn to do all this?"

"Navy. I went through some medical training." He helped her to her feet, grabbing hold of her waistband again. The skin on her lower back was smooth and warm. He wondered if her panties matched her bra. He had always been a sucker for those lingerie ads.

He shook his head, disgusted with his thoughts. He must be more hung up on her than he'd thought to be considering jumping her bones on the way to the hospital. "Next stop, Redwood City emergency room."

Since the accident and Jimmy's death he'd been numb, unable to feel any real emotion, but taking care of her this afternoon had changed that.

He wasn't sure he was ready.

She twisted until she could get up on her tiptoes and kissed his cheek. "Thank you for coming to my rescue."

The sisterly kiss sent a zing through his system. "No problem," he said and led her out to his truck, knowing his comment was probably the biggest lie he had ever told.

His instincts had always been good. This woman could cause him plenty of problems, the kind he had never dealt with before.

The kind that involved his heart.

Chapter Two

Exhausted and fighting tears, Julie stood on the sidewalk beside Tony and contemplated the steps leading to her front door.

They reminded her of Mount Everest.

He had a firm grip on the upper part of her left arm. At least he was no longer hauling her around by the back of her pants.

"Thank you. For everything." She tried to pull away from his big warm hand. She wanted to get in the house before she fell apart. The last thing she wanted to do was cry in front of him.

Tony didn't let go. "Let's get you in the house."

She looked up at the dark windows. "Thanks, but I've taken enough of your time."

He ignored her and urged her up the stairs. "I'll help you get settled."

She didn't want to be rude after he had rescued her, but she needed to be alone. She never let anyone see her cry.

Through the haze of medication that didn't quite block

the pain, she was beginning to realize she wouldn't be able to work on the house for quite a while. The doctor had trussed her up like a Thanksgiving turkey, with her arm in a sling strapped to her chest to immobilize her broken collarbone.

She couldn't finish fixing up the house on her summer vacation.

The utter frustration of her situation overwhelmed her and she groaned. At least her anger at herself helped overcome the urge to cry.

Tony dipped down until his face was level with hers. "Julie? What's wrong?"

If she'd had a good hand, she would have smacked him. What wasn't wrong?

She shook her head. This experience had turned her into a shrew. "Let's just get in the house."

Tony opened the door, flipped on the light in the foyer and led her across the threshold.

She needed to get him out of the house. She just wanted to go to bed and wallow in misery for a while. Tomorrow she'd think about what she was going to do.

"I really appreciate everything you've done. I'd like to pay you for your time."

He looked amazed at her comment, then his mouth thinned into a grim line. "Pay me? You're not in L.A., lady. Folks in small towns help each other."

His angry attitude took her by surprise. She didn't need to be reminded she wasn't in L.A. Stiffly she said, "I'm sorry. I didn't mean it as an insult."

She just wanted him out of the house so she could fall apart. "I've taken up enough of your time."

"My time isn't your problem. Come on, I told you I'm staying until you're settled." Gently, his touch a contrast to his voice, he grasped her arm and started toward the stairs.

Immediately she stiffened up, anger catching up with distress. Getting rid of him was starting to look as tough as getting gum off the bottom of a shoe. Digging in her heels, she decided to be direct. Hinting hadn't worked. "I'm fine. You don't need to stay."

Tony dropped her arm and studied her for a moment. "So, you're fine, huh?"

She nodded. "Yes," she said through gritted teeth.

"How are you going to get undressed?"

Julie hadn't thought about that. Her chin came up. "I'll manage."

He took off his hat and tossed it onto the knob on top of the banister. "How are you going to get your bra off?"

Good question, she thought, feeling slightly embarrassed. How was she going to get undressed? One arm was strapped to her chest and she couldn't bend the other at the elbow because of the stitches.

He threw her a smug look that irritated her. "Do you have any female friends in town?"

She hadn't made close friends except for Lynn, and she lived in New York now. When she'd been sent to live with her grandmother after her parents died, she'd resented being yanked from her home and friends in L.A. and been pretty much of a loner all through high school.

The only person who came to mind was Betty, Lynn's mother. She'd heard Betty was off visiting her son in New Mexico.

"No." Darn him. At least now she was so angry she no longer felt like crying.

"Come on," he said briskly, urging her up the stairs. "Things are going to look much better when you get a little sleep."

Julie didn't think she had ever met a guy who seemed to relish being in control the way Tony did. It rankled. She was used to taking care of herself.

Most of the time.

A little voice in her head reminded her she wasn't doing such a good job.

Her collarbone ached and her stitches burned. Lacking the energy to fight him any longer, she gave in and let him lead her into her old bedroom.

The chair lay there on its side, surrounded by the ledgers.

"What do you sleep in?" he asked matter-of-factly, ignoring the mess.

"There's a nightshirt in the top dresser drawer."

He left her side to rummage through the drawer and came up with a pink flannel nightshirt with the words Uppity Woman scrawled across the front in red. "This?"

She nodded and he laid the shirt over his arm and came back to stand in front of her. With sure fingers he unbuckled the strap around her middle that held the sling close to her body.

"I'm going to take the sling off. I need you to do nothing. Concentrate on keeping your arm perfectly still, okay?"

Julie nodded. That shouldn't be hard. It hurt when she moved even a little.

He slipped the sling off. "You doing okay?"

"Yes." For all his muscles he had a gentle touch.

"Now I'm going to unbutton your shirt." His big hands were quick with the buttons.

For the second time today he had his hands inside her blouse, she thought. It was getting to be a habit.

He slid the shirt off her left shoulder and eased it over her left arm, past the wide elastic bandage covering her stitches.

"Now, let me do all the work here. You just think about holding still." He slid the shirt off her right shoulder and eased it down her arm.

She sighed when he had it off. He had such warm, careful hands. Slick as a whistle, he hadn't hurt her at all. She glanced down to see her nipples puckering through the blue satin of her bra. She wanted to be as cool about this as he was, but her body wasn't cooperating.

Keeping his eyes on her face as if he couldn't be bothered to look at all the skin he'd just uncovered he said, "Turn around."

His voice sounded low and husky.

He wasn't quite as detached after undressing her as he'd like her to believe. Good, because she wasn't detached at all. Obediently she turned.

He stood so close behind her she could feel the heat of his body on her bare back.

He unclasped her bra and slid the straps down her shoulders, over her elbows and her hands, then dropped it like it was a poisonous snake.

Her heart thudded in her chest. What was wrong with her? She barely knew the man and she wanted to feel his hands on her.

It must be the pain medication.

"You're doing fine." His breath feathered the hair behind her ear.

She shivered.

"Cold?" He reached around her from behind to slide her right arm into the sleeve. The back of his hand grazed her bare breast.

He cleared his throat. "You'll be covered up in just a minute."

She was anything but cold. He brought the shirt behind her back and gently eased the fabric over her stiff elbow.

"Okay, turn around." Hands on her shoulders again, he turned her toward him.

She looked up into his face as he did up her buttons and had the oddest sensation of being a desirable woman and a cared-for child all in the same moment.

He eased her into the sling and strapped her up, then stepped back. "There. All set." He was back to his matter-of-fact tone again.

She kicked off her shoes. Julie wanted to hear the husky desire in his voice she'd heard before.

A little devil in her made her say, "Help me with my jeans?" Besides, she thought, how was she going to get the snug denim off without help?

She could see beads of sweat on his upper lip just before he leaned over and fumbled under her nightshirt for the fastener on her pants. His position gave her a great view of his hair, thick, dark and slightly wavy.

He eased the zipper down, hooked his thumbs into the waistband and slid the denim over her hips. She could feel the trail of heat down her body left by the touch of his hands.

He backed up and heaved a sigh as she stepped out of her pants.

"Anything else?" He rubbed the heel of his hand over his chest as if he was in pain.

Julie looked down at her bare toes, hiding a smile. Just one more thing before she let him off the hook. "Ah, my, ah…panties."

She glanced up at him and swore she saw his eyes cross for an instant. It was all she could do not to smirk.

"Sure." His voice was gruff. He reached up and hooked his work-roughened fingers over the elastic and slid the satin down her legs.

Satisfied he had been punished enough for being so controlling, she kicked the panties over with her jeans. "Thanks."

He skirted around her as if she was on fire and pulled the covers down on the bed. "Get in. I'll go get you a glass of water."

He pulled her prescription of pain pills out of his shirt

pocket and smacked the bottle down on the bedside table before he left the room.

Awkwardly Julie scooted under the covers. She lay back against the pillows and thought about what she'd just done. It was petty to harass Tony like that, but people who thought they knew best annoyed her. Plus, she was so angry at herself for fouling up all her summer plans she'd taken out her anger on him.

She supposed she needed to apologize, but she didn't know how to do that without embarrassing both of them.

One more thing she would have to deal with in the morning, she thought as her eyes slid closed.

Tony came back with a glass of water and found Julie had fallen asleep. He pulled the covers up to her shoulders, turned out the overhead light and switched on a small lamp on the dresser across the room.

He wasn't going to wake her up to give her a pill to make her sleep.

He didn't want her awake.

Getting her undressed had been harder than most of the missions he'd been on for the Navy.

He picked up the scattered ledgers and righted the chair. Then he draped her jeans and shirt over the chair, along with the blue bra and matching panties. Her clothes were still warm and smelled like her. With a groan he settled into an overstuffed chair and watched her sleep. She looked so young and innocent lying there.

Hah, he thought. About as innocent as Eve when she teamed up with the serpent in the Garden of Eden.

And he wanted a bite of the apple.

The woman knew just what caliber ammunition she carried. She thought it was safe to mess with his head because she'd been injured.

She was right.

There was time, and Tony was a patient man. She needed him because she wouldn't be able to work on this place for weeks. By the time he had the house in shape and Julie had mended, he planned to show her what happened when you played with fire.

Tony dozed off with a smile on his face.

Chapter Three

Julie woke after a restless night. She felt like she'd been hit by a truck. Groaning, she tried to lift her hand to rub her gritty eyes, but she'd forgotten her arm was strapped to her waist. She tried her other arm and found her elbow so stiff from the stitches she couldn't reach up.

She closed her eyes and fought back frustration, furious with herself for being so clumsy. Her plans to get the house fixed up to sell during her vacation would be on hold for at least a few weeks, if not longer.

Her wonderful timetable was ruined, her dreams on hold.

A tear leaked out from under her lids. She was about to give herself a talking to for being such a weakling when she heard her bedroom door creak.

Before she had time to be frightened, Tony stuck his head in the room.

He grinned, managing to look bashful and incredibly handsome at the same time.

"I didn't want to wake you."

Quickly she turned her head and wiped her eyes on the

pillow case. No way was she going to let him catch her crying like some wimpy little female. He walked in and brought the smell of fresh coffee with him as he handed her a steaming mug.

"Ah," she closed her eyes and drank in the aroma. "You stopped for coffee. Thanks."

She sat up and used her feet to scoot herself against the headboard.

She frowned as she noticed the coffee was in a mug from her grandmother's kitchen.

"Where did you get the coffee?"

He grinned at her again. "Out of the coffeepot."

Besides being extremely good-looking, the man had a killer grin. She wished he would stop using it. It ruined her train of thought.

Julie guided her thoughts back to the conversation. "I have a coffeepot?"

Tony nodded. "In the cupboard above the sink."

She really hadn't paid much attention to the kitchen. "And ground coffee?" Her grandmother had been a tea drinker as far as she remembered.

He shrugged his wide shoulders. "I did have to go to Valley Grocery for that."

Julie peered at the travel alarm clock beside the bed. "How long have you been here?"

"All night."

Oh, swell, she thought, noticing for the first time he had the same clothes on he'd worn yesterday.

That would give the town gossips something to chew on. She'd known him less than two days and he stays over. "I thought we agreed you were leaving," she snapped.

Tony didn't look the least bit upset at her annoyed tone. "I told you I was staying. You might have needed something in the middle of the night."

Vaguely Julie recalled Tony coming to check on her, but

she'd been so groggy from the pain pills she had no idea what time it might have been. And since when did she care what the neighbors might think?

She realized she liked knowing he'd been there and it made her temper rise. She hadn't expected him to stay and she didn't want to impose. She could take care of herself.

"Well, thanks," she said grudgingly. "That was nice of you. But I don't want to keep you from your work."

"No problem. It's raining and I can't work on my house today."

She glanced out the window and noticed the storm for the first time. "Don't you have a regular job?"

"No. I'm building a house on my land."

She wanted to ask how he managed that without regular employment, but didn't know how to do it without sounding like she was prying.

Tony raised an eyebrow and the corners of his mouth turned up in a sly little smile. "Need help getting dressed?"

Obviously he'd recovered his composure after the teasing she'd given him last night. It was her turn to blush. "Ah, I think I can manage."

"The doctor said you can leave the sling off during the day. You just have to be careful."

Good thing, she thought. There was no way to get out of the nightshirt trussed up the way she was.

He turned and headed out her bedroom door. "I'll wait for you downstairs. Give me a yell if you need help."

Julie sipped on the coffee and pondered her options. She could drive back to L.A. or stay here until she healed. Then she remembered her apartment had been sublet for the summer and her car had a stick shift. No way could she make the twelve-hour drive home even if she did have a place to live.

Okay, she would stay here in Ferndale. She scooted to

the side of the mattress and wiggled around until she got her feet on the floor.

There had to be things she could do to the house one-handed, so the next few weeks wouldn't be a total loss. Julie finished the coffee, feeling better now that she had the start of a plan in her mind.

She struggled out of the sling and awkwardly managed to get into a pair of panties and sweats. A bra was out of the question, and so apparently, was brushing her hair and putting on socks. She could ask Tony's help with the socks, and even her hair, but she would have to go braless. There was no way she'd ask him for help with that.

Remembering the way she had acted last night brought a blush to her face. She must have been out of her mind to tease him like that. She barely knew him. Maybe she could blame her behavior on the pain medication she'd taken on the way home.

She made her way downstairs and found Tony sitting in the kitchen, slicing into a coffee cake.

She inhaled the smell of cinnamon and nutmeg, her mouth watering. "Tell me you did not bake that this morning."

He laughed. "No. Mrs. Smithy dropped it off."

Julie didn't recognize the name. "Why?" Why would someone bring Tony a freshly baked coffee cake at her house?

He slipped a wedge of cake onto a plate and pushed it across the table towards her. "Because she heard you had been hurt in an accident.

Julie searched her memory. "I don't even know who she is."

"I think she knew your grandmother. Besides, this is a small town. Folks do nice things for each other in small towns."

He'd made it very clear yesterday that he thought small

towns were highly preferable to large cities. He saw this gift of food as a good thing.

Julie frowned, looking down at the plate. She viewed it as an intrusion into her privacy. By now everyone in town probably knew that she had been clumsy enough to fall off a chair.

The coffee cake smelled so good she decided not to let the reason it was in the middle of the kitchen table get in her way of enjoying it. She set her socks, brush and a rubber band down on the chair beside her and settled in to savor some home baking. Awkwardly she forked up a mouthful.

Tony watched her uncoordinated movements and nodded in approval. "The more you use that arm the less stiff you'll be."

She smiled at him. "Thank you, Dr. Tony."

He cut a huge piece of cake for himself and sat across the table from her. After he had demolished half his piece of cake he paused and cleared his throat.

Julie glanced up, waiting. Obviously he was working his way up to saying something.

Finally he said, "Julie, I know you wanted to do all the work on this house yourself, but you aren't going to be able to manage for a while. Why don't you hire me? I could use the money."

She was tempted. By hiring him she could get done even sooner that she had first planned and get back to L.A. Even if she hadn't broken her collarbone she had no illusions that she could do the work as well or as fast as someone with experience and skill.

Hiring him would solve part of her problem, but there was a hitch. She hated to admit it, but her plan to do over the house herself was based on a lack of cash.

He had made a nice offer and he deserved an explanation, even though she didn't want to give him so much personal information.

"I can't afford to pay you and buy materials and supplies. I get paid ten months a year. I'm really strapped for cash."

Tony shrugged one muscular shoulder. "No problem. Pay me when you close escrow. I'm saving money for stock."

"Stock? You play the market?" She couldn't picture him buying and selling, gambling on the stock market. He was too...steady.

He looked puzzled for a minute, then he laughed. "No. Stock as in horses."

"Oh." She felt silly. Hadn't she nicknamed him cowboy? Of course he meant horses.

"When I get my house built, I'll start on the barn and corrals. I'm going to raise and train horses."

Julie studied him for a moment. Horse rancher. It fit. "Let me think about it, okay?"

"Sure." He stood up and scooped up her plate and his, carrying them to the sink. She watched him walk across the kitchen, admiring the fit of his worn jeans. The man did have one fine body.

He finished rinsing the plates and she quickly looked down at her folded hands as he turned toward her.

Tony stopped beside her chair. "I have to go check on Mrs. Trimball's place, then I'll be back."

Betty Trimball, the minister's widow and the only person in Ferndale she could call a friend, lived three blocks away.

She scooted her chair back across the worn linoleum. "When does Betty get back?" Julie wanted to see her again. There were very few people she felt that way about.

"A couple more weeks." Tony squatted down beside her chair, took hold of her ankle and propped it on his thigh. He drew her sock onto her foot, and repeated the motion as he put on her other sock. The feel of his big square competent hands on her skin sent shivers up her legs.

In one fluid motion he stood up and picked up her brush. He drew the bristles through her hair in steady, firm strokes. Between the warmth of him at her back and the feel of the brush against her scalp, she had to brace herself to keep from sliding out of the chair.

She noticed he was very careful to be gentle over the lump on the side of her head where she had smacked her skull against the floor.

Where had he learned to deal with long hair? she wondered. An unexpected stab of jealousy spiked through her. Why did she even care?

"Ponytail?"

"What?" She tried to get her thoughts back to what he had asked.

"Do you want your hair in a ponytail, or down?"

She almost asked him how he wanted it. Stupid. Why should she care what he preferred?

"Ponytail." She picked the elastic band off the chair beside her and held it up as far as her stiff elbow would allow.

She felt him twist the rubber band around her hair, and then he handed her the brush.

He still had a hold of her hair and he gave it a teasing little tug. "I'll stop by before I head home to see if you need anything."

No one had cared enough to ask her if she needed anything for a very long time. The tears that had snuck up on her earlier threatened to return. It had to be the pain medication. She blinked them back and stood, turning to face him.

"Thank you. For everything."

He shoved his hands into his pockets, shrugged and

dipped his head in an endearing little boy kind of way. "No problem. See you later."

He was out the back door and into the summer rain, leaving her feeling that her thank you had been inadequate considering all he had done for her in the past twenty-four hours.

Julie settled back in her chair and pondered what she should do. If she hired Tony she could get the work done by the time she had to go back to L.A. That way the house would be on the market. If she waited to do the work herself, she would probably have to make at least a few extra trips back up to Ferndale. She wouldn't be able to put the place on the market until late fall, if that soon. With the price of gas and wear and tear on her car for extra trips, it made sense to hire Tony.

The thought made her feel uneasy. It wasn't that she didn't trust him to do a good job. After all, wasn't he building a house all by himself? It was just that she had planned to do it alone. Be her own boss, make her own decisions.

She had already seen him in action. He liked to be in control of a situation.

She began to argue with herself. She would still be in charge. She could help him out as he worked. That would speed things up. He had the skill and expertise, and she could learn from him.

She sat for a long time as her fingers fiddled with the bristles of her brush. Money and control weren't the only problems, she thought.

She was attracted to him.

Very attracted.

If she hired him to work, they shouldn't start a relationship that had nowhere to go anyway. He had made it clear he liked small town living, and in a matter of weeks she would head back to her life in Los Angeles.

She stood up and gingerly stretched her sore muscles,

then headed upstairs, her thoughts still swirling. So the real question was, could she work with him and maintain her distance? Just be friends?

Of course she could.

She'd been around plenty of good-looking men. Even had a few who were friends. She laughed at herself. Was she turning her rescuer into some kind of irresistible knight on a white horse?

He was just a guy.

She set her brush down on the dresser and surveyed the damaged ceiling that she'd stripped yesterday. Just the thought of lifting her arms over her head to apply the plaster made her wince.

Julie made her decision. If she and Tony could come to reasonable terms, the ceiling would be their first project.

The sound of the front doorbell interrupted her thoughts. She headed down the stairs. A middle-aged woman stood on the porch holding a dish covered with foil. Julie thought she looked vaguely familiar but it was hard to tell through the wavy old oval glass window in the door.

She opened the door and the woman smiled. "Julie, I don't know if you remember me. I'm Jane Arnold."

As soon as she spoke, Julie remembered. Jane Arnold had been one of the adults who led the youth group at the church. "Of course I remember." Almost, she thought.

Mrs. Arnold held out a covered casserole. "I heard what happened. I made you some chicken."

Of course. Hadn't she predicted that the whole town would know? Julie remembered her manners. "Won't you come in?"

"Thank you, dear, but I'm on my way to an appointment. Let me just put this in the refrigerator for you."

Julie followed her to the kitchen and then back to the front door, feeling awkward over the woman's show of concern. At Mrs. Arnold's insistence, Julie promised to call if she needed anything.

By the time Tony returned hours later Julie had gotten tired of running up and down the stairs to answer the door and had planted herself in the front room.

"How are you feeling?" he asked, giving her a quick once-over.

His question vaguely annoyed her. She wasn't sure how she felt about him taking on the role of her guardian.

"Tired, but otherwise pretty good." Actually, answering the door had worn her out.

"Take any more pain pills?"

"No." She was trying to avoid them. They made her stupid, and if she was going to be around Tony she needed to stay smart.

"Hungry?"

She thought for a moment. "Yes."

"I'll go get some groceries." He started to turn toward the front door.

Julie grimaced. "Not necessary."

She motioned to him to follow her to the kitchen and opened up the refrigerator. There were five casseroles inside. "I will be eating tuna and noodles and chicken and rice for the next week."

Tony surveyed her newly filled refrigerator and shook his head. "Looks like a church potluck on Saturday night."

"Yeah," Julie remarked sourly. "People just couldn't wait to come and see Julie, all grown up and clumsy."

Tony shot her a startled look, but didn't say anything. He started touching the sides of the casserole dishes, then lifted the foil on the corner of one on the second shelf. "This one is still fairly warm. Want to start with it?"

Why was he being so nice? He couldn't like tuna and noodles that much. "Are you sure you don't have anything better to do?"

"What, and miss a free lunch? No, ma'am." He grinned and pulled the glass dish out of the fridge.

Julie settled down onto one of the chairs and watched him scoop a huge amount of casserole onto a plate. When he started to fill the other plate she said, "Whoa, cowboy. I need less than half of that."

He carried the plates to the table, found some silverware, and sat down. Julie watched, fascinated as he methodically and quickly cleaned his plate.

"Do you always eat that much?"

He shrugged. "Usually. I stay pretty busy during the day."

She shoved the food around her plate. "Speaking of that, I've done a lot of thinking. I'm going to need some help, but I want to make sure you have the time. I mean, that you're not going to regret your offer."

He studied her face. "I wouldn't have made the offer if I didn't want to do it."

She felt herself warm under his direct gaze. "Well, I just wanted to be sure."

"I do need to keep working on my place, so how about I come in three days a week? We'll see how it goes." Tony stood up and carried the dishes to the sink.

"Okay. How long does it take you to get here from where you live?"

"If there's no fog and the road isn't washed out, about an hour and a half."

That was worse than the commute times in L.A. "You're kidding? You live that far out?"

"Have you been down Petrolia Road to the Lost Coast?"

She'd heard of it. "No. My grandmother never allowed me to go. She thought that's where kids went to drink and get into trouble." Besides, she'd been such a loner in high school she'd only been invited once.

Tony grinned at her. "She was right. I've chased kids off my property on occasion."

He came around and helped her as she scooted back out of her chair. "Why don't we take a look at what needs doing."

Stiffly she got to her feet and stretched to get some of the kinks out. "Well, you've already seen the ceiling upstairs."

"You did a nice job of cleaning it up."

"Thanks." She felt a glow of appreciation at his approval.

They wandered through the downstairs rooms, Julie pointing out what she wanted to do, as Tony nodded and added suggestions.

By the time they went upstairs into the room where she slept they'd settled on an hourly wage and Julie had a good idea of how long things would take. She felt better about her decision to hire Tony.

He was so businesslike she felt foolish thinking they would have problems working together.

She wandered over and looked out the window at the backyard, wondering if she should just forget the outside until later. The yard was a mess. Dead bushes and scrubby patches of grass filled the yard, along with the ugly supports for a clothesline that looked like two giant croquet wickets made out of thick galvanized pipe.

If she did any work on the yard now she'd just have to keep it up until the house sold. The yard could wait until the house was finished.

This plan was going to work, she thought as she gazed down on the dead grass and scraggly shrubs. Tony was friendly but businesslike, they agreed on what needed to be done, and paying him when the house sold fit into her tight budget.

Her worries over them having a personal relationship that got in the way of their business had been silly thinking.

Julie turned to mention the yard to him and came up against a very firm male body. She hadn't heard him step behind her.

She lurched back in surprise and lost her balance. He reached out and grasped her around the waist to steady her. She smelled soap on his skin.

Every thought about keeping her distance flew right out of her head.

Tony stared at her for a minute, started to pull her toward him, then mumbling something about tomorrow, turned, and left.

She heard the front door close behind him and promised herself that tomorrow she would keep her distance.

When she got too close he was irresistible, pulling at her like a magnet.

Chapter Four

As Tony pounded through the last of his morning run, his thoughts kept turning to Julie. She seemed like a confident sophisticated woman, but he sensed there was more there, a vulnerability lurking under the surface veneer. Maybe he was just imagining it, but he felt there a lot more to Julie Kerns than she let people see.

That wasn't his problem, he reminded himself. She was his boss now, and it would be best to keep the relationship on a purely friendly level.

Ha! He thought. Easy enough to think, harder to do.

He finished his six-mile run at the highest point on his property just as the sun broke over the horizon. He'd seen this view through Jimmy's eyes long before he'd ever seen it for himself. The sweeping view of the coast never failed to impress him. He'd grown up far from any body of water, and the sight of the Pacific Ocean laid out before him always left him with a feeling of awe.

Even after two years the fact that he owned the land at all still amazed him. He didn't like to dwell on why. Jimmy's death had been painful for him on so many levels.

Tony walked toward his trailer as he cooled down. When they had made out their wills during training, both had had the same attitude. They were golden, nothing was going to happen to them. The next-of-kin thing was just a formality that the desk jockeys thought was necessary.

Tony hadn't had any idea Jimmy had named him as his beneficiary until he had awakened in the hospital a month after the accident. They didn't even tell him Jimmy was dead. Looking back on it, he knew, though. He could tell by the way everyone who came to visit him avoided mentioning Jimmy. When he'd finally had the guts to ask the chief, he'd gotten a straight answer. One that had set him back.

Tony stripped off his shorts and shoes and stepped under the makeshift shower behind the trailer. It might be summer, but it was still cool along the coast. He let a stream of water out of the solar bag hanging from the branch of a tree and almost howled at the cold.

Usually he worked out and showered later in the day, when he was done working. But today he was driving into town to start work on Julie's house, and he wasn't going to go smelling like a goat. Not when she always smelled so good.

He soaped up and remembered the feel of her hair as he had brushed it for her yesterday. She had great hair.

Would she be able to manage a shower by herself? Visions of Julie naked with water streaming over her smooth skin snaked through his mind. Not even the frigid water could prevent the obvious signs that the image invoked. He released more water from the overhead bag in a fruitless effort to cool off his thoughts.

He shook off the water and toweled himself dry before going into his trailer to find clean clothes. He wanted to be at Julie's early enough to put in a full day and still get home in time for some daylight hours to finish the portion of roof over the kitchen.

His truck coughed and sputtered, stalling twice before he got the engine running. On the long drive he thought about the coming months.

He might be able to shower outside now, but by fall it would be too cold. By fall he wanted to be living in his house. He'd sell the trailer and with the money he earned from Julie he could go to the stock auction in Acton and buy the start of his herd.

Tony stopped at the hardware store and the bakery. He pulled up in front of her house and got out of the truck.

She answered the door in a loose terry-cloth robe and a towel wrapped lopsided around her head. It looked like it might slide off if she didn't keep her head tipped to the side.

She had been in the shower.

With difficulty Tony suppressed the images he'd had earlier.

He pointed to the towel. "That doesn't look like it was easy."

She smiled. "No kidding. I practically had to stand on my head."

He followed her into the kitchen, relieved she couldn't see his face. The image almost made his eyes cross. He cleared his throat and changed the subject. "How's the arm?"

She smiled. "Which one?"

He put down the box he carried and took her hand, pushing up the loose terry-cloth sleeve up her arm. His thumb trailed along her smooth skin. The stitches looked tight and the skin around them a healthy pink.

"Looks good. Getting a little more flexible?" His grip tightened on her hand. He wanted to stroke her skin.

She made a little humming noise in the back of her throat

and then pulled out of his grasp. She stepped back and shook her sleeve back into place. "Yes. It still pulls a lot, but I think they'll hold."

The silence stretched between them for a long moment as he watched her cheeks flush a becoming pink.

Tony cleared his throat. "Did you make coffee?" He didn't smell any.

She shook her head at his question. "No. I couldn't reach up high enough to get a filter."

"You get dressed and I'll start a pot. Then I can get going on that ceiling."

"Okay." Julie turned and left the kitchen.

He watched her go. How did she do it? Even in a loose bathrobe the woman looked like a million bucks. Tony turned his attention to the coffee. Down boy, he thought. She's not available for a lot of reasons.

He got the filters down and left them on the counter beside the bag of coffee after he filled the pot and turned it on.

Then he went out to his truck and got the muffins and the rest of the supplies he'd picked up at the hardware store. He put the box of supplies down on the counter, and the bag of muffins on the table.

Julie came back into the kitchen, dressed in an L.A. Lakers T-shirt and a pair of jeans. She had managed to comb her own hair. Tony was disappointed he wouldn't get to do that for her today.

Tony handed her a cup of coffee. "Muffins on the table."

"Thanks." She jerked her head toward the refrigerator. "Sure I can't heat up some tuna and noodles?"

Tony smiled and shook his head. "Still got some left, huh?"

She slid onto a kitchen chair. "Are you kidding? Three more casseroles showed up after you left yesterday. Apparently I'm on the town e-mail loop. You know, it used to be bad the way talk traveled from person to person when I lived here. Now the town tattlers have taken up with technology. I'm willing to bet that your arrival has already been reported." She reached into the bag and pulled out a blueberry muffin.

She sounded disgusted.

He watched her face as she commented on what she obviously thought was a problem. "And that bothers you? That people know I'm here?"

She shook her head "No, of course not. What bothers me is that everyone thinks what I do needs to be broadcast. It's not newsworthy, nor is it anyone's business."

Tony felt relieved to know it wasn't about him in particular. "And that's one of the things you like about living in Los Angeles."

"Yes. I don't even know my neighbors, let alone care about what they're doing."

That statement told Tony a lot. "You think that's a good thing?"

Julie stiffened in her chair and shot him a "don't go there" look. "Let's not put a value judgment on it. It's the way I like to live."

He spread both his hands out palms toward her in a gesture of retreat. "Okay. I wasn't trying to put it down, just want to understand where you're coming from."

Julie got up from the table without saying anything more. Tony cleared the cups and bag from the muffins.

After an awkward silence Julie said, "Do you need me to help you with the plaster?"

He wanted her to rest. He could tell by the way she moved that she was still hurting from her fall yesterday. "Nope. It's pretty much a one-man job. Or one-woman job." He added hastily.

She smiled at his political correctness. "Then I'll wash

down the woodwork in here to get it ready to paint.'' She gestured to the wooden cabinets.

"You need to take it easy.'' As soon as the words were out of his mouth he knew he'd made a mistake.

Her chin came up and she squared her shoulders. "I need to get this house finished and get back to my life.'' Her tone and the stiff set of her shoulders challenged him to disagree.

No way Tony was going to do that. He'd already annoyed her. If she started to overdo, he could only hope the discomfort from her injuries would slow her down.

He shrugged and changed the subject. "I brought some powdered cleaner.'' He reached into the box on the counter and pulled out the container of cleaner. "Do you have a bucket?''

Julie relaxed her stiff stance. "Are you kidding? Bessie was the queen of clean. I think she had a bucket for every day of the week. There's enough cleaning equipment in the cupboards on the porch to last for years.'' She headed out the back door and onto the screened-in porch.

Once again Tony noted the hint of bitterness in her voice when she mentioned her grandmother. He wondered if she realized she sounded that way every time she spoke of the woman. He doubted it. He sensed she didn't like to reveal personal things about herself.

Tony took a bucket from Julie and filled it halfway with warm water in the stationary tub by the back door. He tore open the top of the box of powdered cleaner and dumped some in.

Julie reached for the box. "Don't you need to measure that?''

Reading directions and making calculations was so hard for him since his accident he avoided them and guessed on amounts.

"I use this a lot,'' he fibbed. "That's about right.''

Julie studied the instructions on the box, then shot him a dubious look. "Okay, if you say so."

Tony lifted the bucket out of the sink, carried it to the kitchen and set it on the floor by the cabinets. Then he went back to the cupboard, got another bucket and filled it with warm rinse water.

Julie grabbed a handful of rags and started to work. Tony bit down on his urge to tell her to take it easy. A comment like that might just make her work harder.

He headed upstairs and into Julie's bedroom. First he tidied her unmade bed. The sheets smelled like her. He had the urge to bury his nose in her pillow. Instead he lined up all the materials he needed, unfolded a tarp and started to work. The sounds of old rock and roll tunes drifted up the stairs. He recognized several of the songs as favorites of his parents.

Good music to work to, he mused as he methodically covered the damaged area of the ceiling with patching plaster. His mind kept wandering downstairs but he checked the urge to go and see how Julie was doing.

By the time he finished the patch, his shirt, hair and face were caked with little blobs of plaster. He took the tools he'd been using down the stairs and straight out the front door so he wouldn't track plaster through the house. He went around into the backyard to rinse his tools.

The cracked old hose hooked up to the faucet had holes all along its length, getting him wet. He made a mental note to buy a new one.

He stripped off his shirt and whacked it against one of the uprights for the clothesline to knock off the worst of the plaster, then rubbed his face and hair with it.

Tony eyed the pipe structure. He assumed Julie would eventually take it out. Everyone these days had a dryer and the big ugly thing stood right in the middle of the yard.

He dropped his shirt, reached up and grasped the cross-bar and did a few pull-ups. Maybe he could talk her into letting him dig it up and take it back to his place. He could use it as a wash line and a piece of equipment when he worked out. He had been making do with a tree branch, but this was much better.

Julie heard Tony go out the front door. She threw her rag into the bucket and went to look out the window, but he wasn't in the front yard. She gathered the mail out of the box and flexed her sore left arm as she walked back into the kitchen. The stitches were starting to itch and pull.

Needing a break, she sorted through the flyers and junk mail, tossing everything in the wastebasket.

Movement in the backyard caught her eye. She looked up, there was Tony, naked to the waist, his faded jeans riding low on his hips, doing pull-ups on her grandmother's clothesline.

Her mouth went dry. Every beautifully sculpted muscle in his back and arms stood out as he repeatedly drew himself up until his chin was even with the bar.

Good heavens the man was beautiful, she thought. Pure masculine power radiated from his fit body and made her yearn to run her hands over his torso.

Without thinking she brought her right hand up to her pounding heart. The pain from moving her arm brought her back to reality.

She turned her back on temptation. She was going to have to find a way to tell him to keep his shirt on, or she wasn't sure she could trust herself.

Julie laughed. How was she going to tell him? *Excuse me, Tony, but your body is so fine I don't think I can control myself, so would you please keep it covered?*

"What's so funny?"

She yelped and jumped at the sound of his voice just behind her. She hadn't heard him coming. Too many wicked thoughts must've blocked her other senses.

"Nothing. Really." She chanced a glance over her shoulder and was relieved to see his shirt was back where it belonged. As if covering up that magnificent torso could blot out the memory.

She frantically tried to think of something to say. All she could come up with was, "Are you hungry?"

He stared at her for a long moment, then smiled. "Always."

She'd experienced a hunger for him, but he meant food, she thought, only food. She knew she was blushing, so she hurried over to the refrigerator and opened the door. Staring at the many casserole dishes, she let the cold air wash over her face.

She started to pull out the dish closest to her and winced in pain. Tony's arm shot past her and one-handed the heavy dish out of the refrigerator and onto the counter.

He peeked under the foil. "Some kind of pasta with red sauce."

"Fine. That sounds good. Excuse me." She left the kitchen and went upstairs to the bathroom, where she washed her hands, splashed water on her face and did some deep breathing to get herself under control.

She looked at her reflection in the mirror. "We have a deal," she growled. "No romance. He's my employee and it's temporary."

It was silly, really. She was acting like one of her students. She saw it all the time. Fifteen-year-old girls with crushes. Most of them lasted a week, tops.

Well, she was long past fifteen, and a whole lot smarter. She could handle this.

By the time she got back to the kitchen, he'd set the table and had steaming plates of pasta at each place.

She slid into her chair. "Thanks. This looks good." Actually it looked like one of those nasty canned dinners, but it was hot and ready-to-eat and she wasn't going to complain about anyone else's cooking.

They ate in silence for a few minutes. Julie watched Tony put away a huge plate of pasta in record time. When he sat back in his chair she asked him about his property.

As he described the acreage, a change came over his face. He relaxed and then became rather animated. He described the house he was building and the horses he would buy and breed, then train and sell.

Again Julie wondered how he had gotten the money for the property but couldn't think of a way to ask that didn't sound like prying into something that was really none of her business.

All she could picture was how far out he lived, in the middle of nowhere. How could he stand all that quiet?

She watched him gesture as he talked about a high point of land, and the flexing muscles in his forearm reminded her of the sight of him doing chin-ups on her grandmother's clothesline post. Her thoughts detoured to the memory of his naked back.

Finally she realized he was asking her a question.

"So, shall we go up to your bedroom?"

She stared at him, then reined in her lurid thoughts. *He* had been talking about the plaster job he was doing.

"Sure, right." She slid her chair back across the worn linoleum and stood up abruptly. She headed for the stairs, her face on fire as she blushed at her first thought to his mention of her bedroom.

"It must be the pain pills," she muttered.

"What?" He was right behind her.

"Nothing." She said over her shoulder.

And she was sticking to that.

Nothing but business where Tony was concerned.

Chapter Five

Julie forced herself out of bed at seven after a very restless night. She would have loved to get more sleep, but she'd figured out Tony was an early riser. He was sure to be at her front door within the hour.

She had done too much yesterday scrubbing down the woodwork in the kitchen and she hadn't finished even a quarter of it. Her broken collarbone had throbbed all night.

Finally she'd gotten up and taken a pain pill, only to have wild wicked dreams of Tony when she had gotten back to sleep.

Then she'd awakened several times to what sounded like noises downstairs, almost as if someone was trying to get in through the back door. She couldn't tell if she was dreaming or really hearing a noise.

After finally getting up her courage, she'd gotten up, armed herself with a hammer and crept downstairs. She'd found no sign of anyone.

Then she'd been awake for what seemed like hours. It was too quiet. Loneliness seemed to close in on her. She was used to the hum and buzz of the city. There was always traffic, even in the middle of the night.

As she stared at the new plaster on the ceiling, which stood out against the dingy paint that surrounded it, she recalled the way Tony had described his land on The Lost Coast. Even the name sounded lonely, but he was so excited about what he was building. The only thing that had ever made her feel that way was when she was writing stories. When her characters would come to her and she could create a world for them on paper.

Julie staggered into the bathroom and looked at her reflection in the mirror. She looked awful. She struggled out of her sweats and into the shower, praying that Tony would show up and make coffee. The man did know how to make a great cup of coffee.

She was disappointed there was no wonderful aroma of coffee when she came downstairs, no Tony, no muffins. Just the blasted quiet that brought back so many memories of living here that she really didn't want to revisit.

Julie heard the sound of a vehicle pulling up and walked out to look out the front window. She recognized Tony's truck.

She turned and went back into the kitchen and measured water and coffee into the pot, listening for his knock on the door. He'd left the filters and the coffee on the counter for her. Thoughtful of him.

She really should give him a key, she thought, so if she happened to be out he could get in to work. Actually she was probably one of the few people who locked their door in Ferndale, but she had lived in the city long enough for it to be a habit.

The coffee began to run into the pot, and still no knock on the door. Julie went back to the front window and saw Tony with his head under the hood of his truck, both arms delving deep into the guts of the vehicle.

Not a good sign.

She opened the door and went down the front walk to stand on the sidewalk.

"Trouble?"

He pulled his head out and looked over at her. "Morning. Yeah, kept stalling on the way in."

He looked as tired as she felt. "Do you know much about engines?" she asked.

"Some. I've checked the obvious things and can't see what's causing it." He slammed the hood closed and gave her a closer look. "Bad night?"

She shook her head. She was not about to admit to him she had overdone things yesterday, so she teased him instead. "No. Why? Do I look bad?"

Tony laughed as he followed her up the walk. "No way am I touching that question."

They both walked around the rotten boards on the porch steps and into the front room. "Ah, coffee. I'm going to wash up." He held up his greasy hands and headed out to the sink on the porch.

They settled down at the kitchen table to discuss the day's work.

"I need to sand the plaster and apply a finish coat. Then I think I should work on your porch next. Someone could get hurt falling through those boards."

Julie nodded. She'd been worried the porch was a lawsuit waiting to happen. "Can you get the wood you'll need here in Ferndale?"

"Cliff should have a supply on hand. It's a fairly simple job to pry up the bad stuff and cut new boards. Then I'll prime and paint."

Quickly she calculated the hours that would take him. "No. You do the wood and I can paint."

He raised an eyebrow. "You feel up to it?"

"Sure," she lied. Her shoulder ached like a bad tooth. But it should be better tomorrow. Or the next day.

She gestured to the kitchen cupboards. A clear line of demarcation showed where she had stopped scrubbing. "I'll finish scrubbing down the kitchen and then I can start painting."

"How about colors? Have you picked them out yet?"

Julie looked around the kitchen. It was a faded, dingy off-white. "I want to stick pretty close to this color so I only have to do one coat. Maybe a cream color."

Tony nodded. "Good idea. How about the porch? Want me to pick up the paint to match when I get the lumber?"

"Sure."

"Want to come to the hardware store with me?"

Julie glanced down at her faded T-shirt and baggy cotton shorts. She had no makeup on, had barely gotten a comb through her hair this morning and wasn't wearing a bra. "I think I'll pass. But if you could pick up some paint chips in cream colors, that would be great."

Tony got up and took his mug to the sink, then turned to face her. "Will do. Anything else?"

You could kiss me. The thought just popped into her head.

She blinked and said, "Can't think of a thing."

"You need a hose."

No, I need a kiss. "I do?"

"Yeah. The one out back is full of cracks and holes."

"Okay, a hose. Get a cheap one, okay?"

"You bet, boss." He threw her one of his killer grins and got up. "Shall I start an account for you with Cliff? I'll keep all my receipts."

He made it sound as if she didn't trust him. It was herself she didn't trust, and it had nothing to do with money. She had pegged Tony as an honest man as soon as she had met him. Just a feeling, but she was sure.

"Well?"

She jerked her attention back to what they had been discussing. "Sure, that would be fine."

"Okay. Be back soon."

As she rinsed their coffee cups in the sink she heard Tony's truck start with a rattle and a cough. It definitely sounded like he had some kind of mechanical problem.

Julie tuned the radio in the kitchen to one of the few stations that she could get and went to fill the bucket. She put it in the sink, measured in the cleaner and added the proper amount of hot water. Then she found she couldn't lift it out of the sink.

Well, shoot. She didn't want to wait for Tony, and besides, she didn't want to admit she couldn't handle something as simple as a bucket. She found a second bucket and used the measuring cup to scoop the cleaner out until she could lift the bucket out of the sink.

As she scrubbed one-handed, she heard the clatter of lumber being dropped on the porch. She listened for the sound of Tony working, but all she heard was quiet.

Finally her curiosity got the better of her and she walked to the front of the house. A stack of lumber blocked the steps, but he was gone and so was his truck. Odd. She thought he was going to come back and go right to work.

Julie went back to scrubbing and finally she heard someone on the porch. Again she waited to hear Tony working and there was no sound.

For the second time she walked to the front room. There was a big can of paint and a brown paper bag on the porch, but no Tony and no truck.

What the heck was he doing?

Once more she went back to washing down the cabinets. She glanced at the clock and wondered if she was going to have to pay him for all the time he was taking to get the supplies. He must have gone someplace besides the hardware store, but Julie couldn't think where. There just weren't many other places to shop in Ferndale for building materials.

Finally she heard the sound of a saw. She put her sponge in the bucket and took off her gloves.

Tony was out on the front yard sawing a length of board. She stepped out on the porch.

He finished making the cut he was working on and turned off the saw, then peeled off his safety goggles.

She glanced up and down the street. "Where's your truck?"

"It crapped out in front of the hardware store. Jim Dooley is going to look at it today."

She vaguely remembered the name. Jim Dooley was a mechanic who worked at the only gas station in Ferndale. "How did you get all this stuff here?"

"I made a couple of trips."

"You mean you walked?"

"Sure. It's only a few blocks. It was a good workout."

"If you say so," she said, unconvinced. To Julie a good workout was an hour on the treadmill at the gym. But then, she didn't have biceps that looked like Tony's. That darned image of him doing pull-ups on her wash line flashed through her mind.

Julie wanted to stay and chat, but she was paying him by the hour. "I better get busy."

She went back into the house and continued to scrub until her collarbone ached so much she had to stop. Her restless night was catching up with her.

She pulled a casserole out of the refrigerator and didn't even bother to look under the foil cover. She was tired and hungry and would eat whatever it was. She turned on the oven and slid the foil covered dish in.

She went upstairs, took a pain pill and curled up on her bed for a minute to rest.

The next thing she knew, the mattress beside her dipped down and she opened her eyes to find Tony sitting beside her, smoothing her hair away from her face. Something smelled like air freshener.

Groggy, she realized the smell obviously wasn't Tony. He smelled like sawdust and man.

"You okay?" He looked concerned.

Julie was touched that he would be concerned about her. "Sure. Just a little tired."

"Need a pain pill?"

"No. I'm fine." She wasn't going to admit she'd taken one. She didn't want to listen to him telling her she was overdoing.

"Hungry?" He smiled, then chuckled.

What was so funny about lunch? "It should be ready. I stuck it in the oven." She turned her head to see the travel clock by her bed. "A half hour ago."

He stood up and laughed again. What the heck was so funny? Julie pushed herself to a sitting position.

He rubbed the back of his neck with one hand. "Did you look to see what it was?"

She shook her head. "No. More tuna and noodles?"

"Actually, this one was Jell-O."

Julie groaned. *That* was the fruity smell. She knew next to nothing about cooking, but she was sure you ate Jell-O straight from the refrigerator.

"I did find some kind of chicken and noodles and put it in the oven. It should be ready by the time you get downstairs."

Julie wished she had brought her microwave with her. Bessie had never allowed one in the house, claimed she didn't trust them.

Tony left the room and she got to her feet, found her sandals and gingerly ran a comb through her hair.

By the time she got downstairs, Tony was serving up the plates.

Julie looked down at the starchy bland mound of casserole on her plate. "This is the last time I can eat comfort food," she said, moving the noodles around with her fork. "What am I going to do with all the stuff in the refrigerator?"

Tony leaned across the table. "We can sneak it out to the garbage can after dark," he said in a conspiratorial whisper. "Fill up all those cottage cheese containers that Bessie stored in the cupboard on the porch and drop them in all the neighbors' cans."

Julie laughed at his dramatics. He was right. Bessie had apparently saved every food container she'd ever emptied. "I'll get on it after lunch." She never wanted to see a casserole again. She was starting to long for a salad.

Tony got up and took their plates to the sink. "See you later."

Now that the pain pill had kicked in, Julie planned to take advantage of it. She pulled all the casserole dishes out of the refrigerator and scooped the contents into the old containers. Bessie must have lived mainly on cottage cheese.

Julie stopped scooping for a moment as the thought hit her. She felt as if she was living in a stranger's house. She'd lived here for four years, and didn't feel as if she had ever gotten to know her grandmother. The thought made her sad for both of them.

The screech of boards being ripped from the porch drew her attention. She shook off her maudlin thoughts and went to work on the dishes. Some were marked with people's names and could be returned. Some were not. She racked her brain and was finally able to match all but two of them to their owners. She didn't relish the thought of returning them. She'd had her fill of neighborly chitchat.

Washing and drying one-handed was a tedious chore and took far longer than she had hoped. Just as she finished, Tony came in for a glass of ice water and announced he was going to check on his truck. "Want to take a walk?"

She looked down at her damp, rumpled shirt. "No, I think I'll just stay here."

"Need anything?" He asked as he left the kitchen.

She eyed the stack of casserole dishes. *I need to get out of this small town.*

"No," she told him as he left.

Julie didn't want to think about returning the dishes. Maybe she could ask Tony to do it on his way home. Then she could avoid all the conversations she didn't want to have. It was the chicken's way out, but she would do it if he was willing.

After a short time she heard the sound of hammering on the front porch. When she looked out the window, there was still no truck. She opened the front door and watched as Tony pounded furiously on one of the new boards.

"Bad truck news?" she asked as he paused for a moment to position a new nail.

"No truck news yet. He can't find the problem. I'll go back in a couple of hours."

Julie thought about her sporty little car, now useless to her.

"You could use my car."

He looked surprised. "Well, thanks. That's a nice offer, but I couldn't get down the road to my property in that low-slung little car. The rocks and high places in the road would rip the bottom out. I need four-wheel drive to get home."

"The road to your house isn't paved?"

He grinned. "The road to my house isn't even gravel for the last five miles."

Why anyone would choose to live in such an inaccessible place was beyond her, but she refrained from saying anything. They had already been over this territory.

He must have read her expression, though, because he said, "Cuts down on door-to-door salesmen."

She shook her head. "Well, I'm glad there's an advantage." She would rather put up with the salesmen.

Julie went back to scrubbing and Tony came in several times for water and a snack. Julie got the impression he was checking up on her.

She didn't know how she felt about that.

Around four he announced he was going back to check on his truck. She went upstairs and changed into a dry shirt. Her stitches were itchy but not so stiff, but her shoulder still ached.

Tony was back by the time she got downstairs. One look at his face was enough to tell her the news wasn't good.

"Dooley thinks I blew a head gasket."

"Is that bad?"

"Oh, yeah."

"How bad?"

"He can't do the work. He'll have it towed into Redding. It'll be days before it's fixed."

Before she had time to even think, the words were out of her mouth. "You want to stay here?"

He looked as surprised at the offer as she was that she'd made it. "You sure?"

"Yes, I'm sure." Actually, when she thought about it, Tony staying at the house made sense. He could get more work done if he didn't have to make the long drive back and forth to his place.

"I was thinking Betty probably wouldn't mind if I slept in her garage."

"Her garage?" Why would he even consider sleeping in a garage?

"Well, I am looking after her place, but I wouldn't use her house without her permission."

"Don't be silly. There is a perfectly good bed down the hall. You can stay here." She repeated the invitation, trying to convince herself as much as him it was a good idea.

"Okay, if you feel comfortable with that. People are going to talk."

She was far from comfortable with the impulsive idea, but she wasn't going to admit it. "If I know Ferndale, people are already talking."

Tony laughed. "Yeah, they are. I've got a sack of laundry that I was going to do on my way home tonight. I'll go and take care of that so I'll have clothes."

"Bring it here. There's a washer on the porch, and the clothesline out back."

He grinned at her. "My boxers on your clothesline might be too much for this town. I'll stop at the Laundromat and while my clothes are being washed I'll go to Valley grocery and pick up some food. What are you hungry for?"

"Mmm, salad."

"See you later."

"Sure you don't want to use my car?"

"Nope. It's only a few blocks."

That was the trouble with Ferndale, Julie though. The whole town was only a few blocks. As he left, Julie realized how relieved she was that Tony was staying.

She didn't like the feeling.

She didn't *need* him here, she told herself. She was just lonely and she missed having someone to talk to.

Chapter Six

Julie couldn't believe she had invited Tony to stay over.
She struggled to brush out a tangle in her hair she couldn't
quite reach. The invitation had just sort of popped out of
her mouth.

Oh, she could come up with reasons. She had been
spooked last night at the scratching noises, and he did need
to stay in town until his truck was repaired. She couldn't
let him sleep in Betty's garage.

It wasn't like her to be so impulsive. But if he stayed
she wouldn't feel so alone. She knew the noises she had
heard last night were probably nothing, but she would sleep
better if Tony was in the house.

Finally she put down the brush and pulled her sweatshirt
down where it had ridden up. It was too hot for sweats, but
she had been self-conscious in a T-shirt and no bra. Not
that her breasts were all that large, she just wasn't used to
going around without underwear. It made her feel undressed.

Julie went downstairs and found two bags of groceries
on the front porch.

He was at it again.

He refused to take her car, but he was making trips back and forth to carry all the stuff he had to lug back to her house.

Tony was the most physical person she had ever met.

Gingerly she lifted a paper bag by the handles. She brought them in one at a time, but couldn't lift them onto the counter.

She was so tired of being debilitated. One-handed, she unloaded the bags. Along with a head of romaine, tomatoes and a cucumber, there was a huge steak, French bread, a toothbrush, toothpaste, a bar of soap and a disposable razor.

She put the food in the refrigerator and left Tony's things on the counter. She eyed the little pile of toiletries and had to laugh. She had ten times that amount of stuff in the bathroom, and considered all of it essential.

It was so much easier to be a guy.

She went upstairs to check that there were sheets on the bed in the room where he would sleep and put out a towel for him in the bathroom.

A bathroom they would have to share.

She took some of her more personal items off the counter and put them in a drawer. A girl needed secrets, especially when she was just going to be friends with the guy.

She heard Tony knocking at the front door and made her way down to let him in. He held an olive-green duffel bag and another sack.

"Hi." He smiled and brushed past her, bring the scent of wood shavings and sweat with him.

She liked the combination. "Get everything?"

He nodded. "Mind if I take a shower?"

"Of course not." Suddenly shy, Julie pointed toward the stairs. "You can use the front room. Third door on the right."

"Okay, thanks." Tony took the stairs two at a time. "I'll be down to fix dinner in a few minutes."

Julie wandered into the living room and picked up the book she was reading. She wouldn't be much help in the kitchen, so she settled down to read.

Tony appeared in the doorway in what seemed like five minutes. "Are you hungry?"

Julie thought for a moment. "Not terribly. Why?"

"You've been cooped up here. Want to go for a drive?"

How thoughtful of him. Getting out sounded very appealing. "Sure."

She got up and dug the car keys out of her purse and tossed them to Tony. "Where are we going?"

"Just down to the beach. We can make it in time for the sunset."

He helped her into the car and then came around and slid behind the wheel. His knees were practically up under his chin. He quickly found the little lever at the base of the seat to adjust for his longer legs.

Tony reached across the console and her, and grabbed the latch for her seat belt. The movement brought his chest up against her shoulder and the smell of clean man made her want to lean into him and breathe deeply. It was almost as good a smell as the sweat and sawdust.

He pulled out the seat belt and drew it across her body, his hand warm at her hip. He pushed the latch into the buckle with a click.

"Okay, now we're ready." He said, very matter-of-factly.

Julie took a breath and nodded, hoping her pulse would return to normal quickly and her face was not too flushed.

Tony drove very competently and very fast once he got out of town. She enjoyed the feel of the road rushing past. She'd never been a passenger in her own car.

She glanced over at Tony, whose full concentration was

on the road, then down at the speedometer. He was going twenty miles over the posted limit.

"Had a lot of tickets?" she asked in a dry voice.

He studied her face for a moment, then smiled. "My share. Want me to slow down?"

"Not on my account." She was thoroughly relishing the ride.

They took the winding road down to the beach and he parked in a little lot at the edge of the sand.

They were the only ones there.

It felt strange to be at the beach and be alone. In L.A. there were always crowds in the summertime, and even in winter there were plenty of people. It seemed like some kind of luxury to have the beautiful stretch of coast all to themselves.

Julie managed to get her seat belt unfastened as Tony came around to open her door. He extended his hand and drew her up and out of the car.

Julie looked up and down the beach. So different than L.A. The beaches there were flat and sandy, and every inch of shoreline had been built on.

There were no buildings here. The sand ran up into a wooded area. And the beach itself was wild and rocky, with dunes and grasses. Much less civilized, but beautiful.

And lonely.

Tony's voice interrupted her thoughts. "Want to walk?"

"Sure." She kicked off her sandals and followed him down onto the sand. When the way got a little rough, he took her hand for a few moments until it smoothed out again. The feel of his warm calloused palm against her smooth skin was pleasant. Almost too pleasant. She didn't want him to let go.

They walked along the shoreline without speaking. Waves broke and crashed out on the surf line, the water rushing toward them to bubble and foam to a halt just shy of where they walked. The smell of salt filled the air and the cry of a fishing hawk was the only sound besides the waves.

No traffic sounds interfered with the magnificence of nature, no cell phones rang, no radios blared.

Julie missed the rattle and hum of civilization she had become so used to. It seemed so isolated here, so lonely.

She tried to understand why Tony liked Ferndale so much. "Do you go in the ocean much?"

"Yeah." He stopped walking and sat down on a huge log that had washed up on the shore, then gently pulled her down beside him.

She settled on the rough seat. The evening sky was painted with brilliant streaks of orange and purple. A couple of curious seagulls stood a few feet away, looking hopeful. Obviously they were used to being fed by people visiting the beach.

"I love to swim and go snorkeling. Surfing, too, but not along here." He gestured to the south. "There are much better beaches than this one for that. You like the ocean?"

"To look at. I'm not much of an ocean swimmer." It was too wild. And cold. She had never liked the way the ocean could toss you around.

They sat in silence and watched the sun slide below the horizon. As soon as the huge ball of fire sank into the water the wind picked up and the evening felt cool.

She shivered as the breeze blew over her wet bare feet. He seemed perfectly comfortable in his T-shirt.

"Ready to head back?" he asked.

"Sure." The walk had done her some good. She actually felt hungry for the first time since she had fallen off the chair. Maybe it was because she didn't have to face a dinner of casserole.

"What has you smiling?" he asked as he pulled her up off the log.

"We're going home to eat and it isn't going to be tuna and noodles."

Tony laughed as he grabbed her hand to help her over a rocky spot. He seemed to reach out to touch her as a natural extension of being together. She wasn't used to being touched so casually. Her dad had been like Tony in that way, and she realized how much she had missed the feel of another person touching her in a simple, caring way. He retrieved her sandals at the edge of the parking lot.

She was glad to settle back in the car. Walking over the uneven ground had jarred her shoulder a bit and it was starting to ache.

They started for home and Tony expertly guided the car over the winding roads, skillfully taking them around the curves.

Her gaze shifted to his big hands on the steering wheel. "Lucky for you there is a very small police presence in Ferndale."

Tony looked over at her and smiled. "Yeah. I know what shifts they work and when they patrol. Makes it handy when I rarely observe the speed limit."

The man took risks, but he calculated the danger. She supposed it was part of the challenge. She had always been a careful person, and this aspect of his personality fascinated her.

They got home and Julie followed Tony into the kitchen.

He turned and studied her face. "Why don't you go and relax? I'll take care of things."

She wasn't going to let him wait on her. "I can at least set the table and show you where things are."

He nodded. "Okay, but I do the cooking and cleanup."

She smiled. "You'll get no argument from me. Want a glass of wine?"

"No, thanks. I'm not much of a drinker."

"And here I thought all you sailors were party boys!"

A look of sadness passed over his features so quickly she almost missed it. She wondered what had caused the emotion, but it was too personal a question to ask. They worked together in silence until Tony had made a salad and broiled the steak.

As they ate they talked about where they had grown up. Tony had a sister and a brother. She had always wanted a sibling. His parents still lived on the piece of property where he was born in Wyoming. Julie had only memories of the house where she had lived until her parents had died.

They cleared the plates and Tony sent her off to rest while he did the dishes. She went into the dining room that her grandmother had converted to a TV room and flipped on the ancient black-and-white television set. She could only get three channels and found nothing to hold her interest, so she went back to her book.

Tony wandered in and announced he was going for a run.

Surprised, she looked up at him. He'd changed from jeans to an old pair of gray shorts. He had long, well-muscled legs.

Julie forced her gaze up to his face. "On a full stomach?"

He shrugged. "I'm not going that far."

He reminded her of some of the boys in her class who seemed to have a difficult time sitting still. She guessed he had been a handful in school with all his energy.

Julie read for almost an hour. It annoyed her that she kept glancing at the clock. Why did she feel she needed to listen for his return? He was a big boy and could take care of himself.

In spite of herself, five minutes later she glanced at the clock again. If this is what Tony considered a short run, she hoped he never invited her along. She could do an hour on the treadmill at the gym at a brisk walk, but she'd collapse if she tried to run for that length of time.

Finally she heard him come in the back door.

He sauntered into the living room. "I'm back." He had his shirt in his hand and he was rubbing at the glistening sweat on his bare chest. Julie's mouth went dry. The muscles he had displayed while doing chin-ups on her clothesline were even better up close. A mat of dark hair covered his chest and sculpted shoulders and arms gleamed in the lamplight.

"I think I'll take another shower, if you don't mind."

"No, go ahead." She would just stay where she was and try not to think about him naked, standing under a spray of water in her old claw-foot bathtub.

On second thought, she decided she needed to keep busy. She hadn't been able to keep her thoughts off him all evening, and with the ammunition he had just added, she knew her mind would wander into dangerous territory if she just sat here.

She decided to get ready for bed. "I'm going to lock up and head upstairs myself."

"You want the bathroom first?"

She kept her eyes on his face. She couldn't take much more. "No. You go ahead."

The man was so fast at getting cleaned up he'd be out of the bathroom before she could check all the doors and windows.

He turned to go upstairs and she stifled a groan. He even had a great butt. Life just wasn't fair. Why couldn't she have hired an ugly guy?

She was right. By the time she got upstairs Tony had finished in the bathroom. He called to her that he was going to bed.

Julie took her turn in the bathroom and then settled down to sleep. She felt reassured that Tony was just down the hall. Whatever had disturbed her sleep last night was not going to bother her tonight with him there in the house.

She drifted off to sleep thinking of how beautiful the lonely beach had been.

She awakened with a start in the dark. She heard the same scratching noise she had heard the night before. It sounded like it was coming from the back of the house, just below her bedroom window. Just as she considered slipping out of bed to wake Tony, a huge form loomed out of the dark, by her bed.

She sat up with a jerk and drew in a gasp of air, preparing to scream. Before she could finishing inhaling a huge palm firmly covered her mouth and pushed her down into the pillow.

Her heart crashed against her chest and she clawed at the hand pinning her down.

He leaned over her and seemed to surround her as he whispered in her ear. "Stay here and don't make a sound."

Through her terror she recognized his voice.

Tony.

His hands slid away from her. And then he was gone.

Heart pounding, she considered what had just happened. She hadn't heard him come into her bedroom. Even though she had been awake, with all her senses on alert. Even though she'd been watching she hadn't seen him leave.

She shivered. How did he do that, she wondered as she strained to hear something, anything from downstairs. There was not a sound. The scratching had stopped and she couldn't hear Tony moving around.

In spite of the fact he had ordered her to stay where she was, she was mustering her courage to get up and investigate. Without a sound, he appeared, a shadowy shape in her bedroom doorway.

"Julie?"

"Yes?" She hated that there was a tremble in her voice. She sounded like a scared little kid. "What was it?"

"I'm going to turn on the light."

She squinted against the bright flare of light. Tony was holding a huge orange-and-white cat.

"Barnaby!" It was her grandmother's cat.

"So, you know him?" Tony scratched Barnaby under his chin and Julie could hear his purr across the room.

She tugged her nightshirt down and slid out of bed, crossing over to Tony. "A friend of Bessie's in Fortuna took him after the funeral."

"Well, I guess he found his way back." Tony continued to scratch him and Barnaby looked like he was going into a near-coma state of pleasure.

He didn't look like the journey had done him any harm. He was still overweight and his coat looked shiny and clean.

Julie eyed the giant feline. "I have to warn you. When he gets this relaxed, he starts to drool. It's one of his more endearing habits."

Tony shrugged and laughed. "What do you want to do with him?"

"I suppose he can stay. If he's going to find his way home like this I don't want to send him back. He might not be so lucky the next time he tries it."

"You want him outside?" Tony stepped back out of her room.

"No. He'll be okay until morning." Julie followed him into the hall.

Tony set Barnaby down and the cat twitched his tail once in an annoyed gesture, then sauntered down the hall as if he owned the place. Which, Julie thought, he had always believed he did. Her grandmother had spoiled him for years.

Julie realized she was standing very close to Tony and

he wore nothing but a pair of boxer shorts covered with cartoon characters. She took a step back toward her room, but curiosity over what has just occurred got the better of her.

She eyed him in the light from her bedroom. "How did you do that?"

He lifted his gaze from the retreating cat and focused on her. "How did I do what?"

She gestured toward her bed. "Come in here and then leave without me seeing you?"

He hesitated then said, "It was dark."

She threw him a skeptical look. "It wasn't *that* dark."

"You were asleep."

"No. I was awake. The noise woke me up." What didn't he want to tell her?

After a long silence he said, "I had some special training in the Navy."

"What kind of training?" Stealth training? Was it a class you could take?

"I was a SEAL. We learned how to get in and out of places without being noticed."

Now there was an understatement. She was surprised he hadn't mentioned he was in Special Forces. "How long?"

He got a faraway look on his face. "Was I in the SEALs? Six years."

"Why did you leave?" As soon as the words were out of her mouth she realized it was a very personal question.

He hesitated so long with his answer she thought he wasn't going to tell her.

"I had an accident. I was no longer fit for duty."

She detected a slight edge of bitterness in his tone. "How long ago?" She persisted even though she could sense his reluctance.

He seemed to gather himself, and his voice was back to his usual casual tone. "Almost two years."

She sensed there was so much here that he was trying to avoid. "Do you miss it?"

He shrugged and in a quick move leaned toward her, neatly trapping her up against the doorjamb. "You smell good."

The abruptness of his move and change of subject made her forget her question. All she could think of was the hard warm body inches from her own. Her nightshirt and his boxer shorts didn't provide much of a barrier. This was *such* a not good idea.

Bracing his hands on the wall, he leaned in further. She could feel his breath against her temple. "Tony, I—"

He cut off her protest with a brush of his lips across hers. She forgot what she was going to say.

His lips settled on hers, warm and firm and oh, so gentle. She leaned into him and he slid one arm around her waist and pulled her against him while his mouth worked some kind of magic on hers.

Without conscious thought she raised her arms to circle his neck and hold him there, and her broken collarbone shot a shaft of pure bright pain straight down her arm.

He steadied her and murmured an apology. "You okay?"

Her sanity returned. "Yes, I'm fine."

"I'll see you in the morning," he said, and walked down the dark hallway as if the last minute had never happened.

Julie turned into her room, switched off the light and crawled into bed.

She lay awake for a long time, staring into the dark and remembering how his lips felt as they'd cruised over hers.

Chapter Seven

"You want to tear it up and see what shape the wood is in?"

Julie jerked her attention away from the memory of the kiss he'd laid on her last night and back to the wooden stairway. He was squatting down on the landing, pointing to the worn carpet.

"You mean leave the steps uncarpeted?"

"Well, this stuff is in terrible condition, and it's going to look worse with new paint on the walls." He stood up and brushed his hands off on his jeans. "You could replace it, but why go to the expense if the wood is in good shape? The new owners can carpet the steps if they don't want it bare."

"Can you pull up a corner so we can check?" she asked, unwilling to commit to a major restoration of the wood.

"Sure. Let's start at the top." He brushed past her and climbed the steps.

Carefully he pried the carpet away from the tack bar and peeled it back while Julie watched from a lower step.

"Looks pretty good. What do you think?"

She thought the way his jeans pulled over his butt was a fine sight when he hunkered down, but she didn't comment on that because *he* was referring to the carpeting.

She peeked at where he was pointing. The wood under the carpet was in better shape than the uncovered wood. "What about the nail holes?"

"Those will be easy enough to fill and sand. Then a coat of stain to even out the color and a top coat and they should look good."

Julie calculated the amount of work. She could manage most of that herself. "Okay. Let's do it."

Tony threw his strength into pulling up the old carpet, and piece by piece, Julie dragged the nasty dusty stuff down the stairs and out the front door.

Julie watched Tony work and thought about last night. His kiss had darn near curled her toes. Strange, because she hadn't been expecting it and it hadn't lasted very long.

She thought back over their conversation leading up to the event. She'd wanted to know how he felt about the accident and leaving the service. Obviously he hadn't wanted to talk about it. So he had distracted her with a kiss.

What an understatement!

There had to be a far better word than *distract*.

How about bewilder? Or befuddle? He'd certainly been effective. She hadn't remembered her unanswered question until this morning.

The guy had quite a technique.

She pulled another hunk of the old carpet out the front door and dumped it on the lawn.

He had so much potential. He was good-looking and personable. With an education he could go far. He said his dream was to have his horses out in the middle of nowhere, but he could have a professional job and still have his ranch.

What was he doing hiding himself out here, in this little town? Not even in the town, she thought. Way outside the town.

Plenty of successful people had weekend places and indulged themselves in their hobby.

Julie dusted herself off and walked back into the house. The trick was to bring the subject up without damaging his male ego. All guys had one, and as far as Julie could tell, most of them were pretty fragile. She'd have to think on this for a while and wait for the right time.

Tony ripped up the last piece of carpet and carried it out past Julie. When he came back in they stood and surveyed the stairs. A thick layer of grit and dirt covered the wood, but as far as she could tell, the stairs were in pretty good shape.

She glanced up at him. Dust covered his shirt and pants. "What do you think?"

"I think you lucked out. The wood is sound, and will only require a minimum of work to make it look pretty good."

"I can take care of cleaning this up if you want to start on something else."

"You sure? I can help you haul the vacuum."

"No. I can handle it. Why don't you get started on the framing around the back door?" The wood had rotted away on the bottom of the frame and the threshold of the door that led out from the porch to the backyard.

He touched her arm briefly. "Okay, but call me if you need any help."

She ignored the little zing of sensation when his hand landed on her skin. "Will do."

Julie started with the broom in an awkward one-handed way and swept clouds of dust down into the entry hall. She wouldn't have been surprised if the dust was fifty years old. The carpet had been there a long time.

As she worked she thought about what she would say to Tony concerning his education. Surely there was some kind of assistance, like the old G.I. Bill, for people coming out of the service who wanted to go to school. He could start at community college and take his general education classes. That would cut down on the expense.

She glanced out the window in the front door and spotted the object of her speculation kneeling on the front lawn, rolling the carpet into neat bundles and tying it up with cord.

Julie rested for a moment on the handle of her broom and watched him work. His movements were economical and spare, efficient.

He was tidy and organized, and she was so glad she had decided to hire him.

As they worked it occurred to her that there was no way she could have done all that needed to be done by herself. What had she been thinking? With her do-it-yourself books and absolutely no skills to speak of?

Julie shook her head and awkwardly scooped as much of the dust as she could manage into a paper grocery bag. She would bring the vacuum in and finish the job after lunch.

Julie wandered into the kitchen, then wasted more time watching Tony haul the last of the rolled carpet through the gate in the back fence and into the alley.

She turned and surveyed the contents of the refrigerator. Normally she would run out and bring in ready-to-eat food, but between how she looked and her new budget restraints, she had made a resolution to save money by eating at home.

That meant they would have peanut butter and jelly. Her grandmother had left a shelf full of jars of homemade jam, and there was a jar of peanut butter in the refrigerator.

Peanut butter lasted forever, didn't it? She searched the jar for an expiration date. Yup, still good.

Julie was trying to decide how to slice the bread left from dinner last night when Tony came in through the back door.

"What are you doing?" He eyed the knife held awkwardly in her left hand.

Frustrated, she snapped at him. "Trying to figure out how to slice bread."

He took the knife gently out of her hand. "You fixing us a gourmet lunch?" He asked gently, teasing her out of her mood as he eyed the jars of peanut butter and jelly.

It wasn't his fault she'd fallen off a chair. She had no right to take her bad mood out on him. She smiled at him. "You bet. Only the best for us."

He put his hand on her shoulder and gave her a gentle push. "Tell you what. I'll put together the sandwiches and you set the table."

"Okay. I can handle that."

They worked together in the kitchen in silence and within moments were sitting down to lunch.

They ate quietly for a while. Julie decided this would be a good time to bring up the subject of education.

"Tony, have you ever considered getting an education so you could get a real job?" As soon as the words were out of her mouth she realized how badly she had started.

He stopped eating and went very still, his only movement a raised eyebrow. "Real job? As opposed to what I do now?"

She knew she should stop, but it was too late to take it back. She forged ahead, carefully picking her words. "I mean a career. You know, get an education and have a career. You could still raise horses. I mean you wouldn't have to give that up."

Tony studied her in a way that made her want to squirm.

Finally he spoke. "Do you have a problem with what I do now?"

"No. Well, only that I think education is important. It opens up all kinds of doors."

"You mean the kind of doors I get to walk through wearing a suit and driving a nice car? Those kinds of doors?"

Julie squirmed in her seat. When he repeated her thoughts so accurately they sounded arrogant. She hadn't meant to make his life sound trivial. "That's not exactly what I meant."

"What *exactly* did you mean?"

She wavered for a moment. "Just that you have so much potential."

"And you think I'm wasting it?" His voice sounded low and ominous.

She swallowed hard, wishing she'd never brought the subject up. "Maybe you're taking the easy way out. You could think about it, couldn't you?"

He continued to pin her with his steady gaze. "Would you be ashamed to introduce me to your friends in L.A.? The ones with the suits and the cars and the education?"

She hesitated for a brief moment, wanting desperately to find the right words. She had done this so badly. "No. Of course not."

Tony put down his sandwich and bunched his fists in his lap, struggling to keep his temper under control.

He hadn't missed her hesitation. What did she think she was talking about? He'd bet that none of the men she knew in L.A. had served their country.

A little voice taunted him. *And none of them had ever gotten their best friend killed, either.*

His anger threatened to swallow him up.

Tony pushed back from the table. "When you're so busy thinking about doing the things I need to do, maybe you should take some time and reexamine your values. Just because I don't wear a suit and work at a high-powered job doesn't mean what I'm building here isn't worthwhile.''

He stood up. ''Is a pile of money in the bank what turns you on? Maybe you should hurry yourself back to Los Angeles.''

She opened her mouth to protest and he cut her off. ''You don't know the first thing about what is really important in life.''

Or how quickly life can go sour on you. He knew. And that was why he was following his dream.

To her credit, she looked guilty. She braced her hands on the table and leaned toward him. ''I think you misunderstood what I was trying to say.''

Tony threw his napkin down beside his plate. She was a snob, plain and simple. He should have realized. ''No. I think I understood very well.''

''Tony, I—''

He cut her off by raising his hands. He could tell her he had an education, but then he'd have to tell her everything else. ''Don't say anything else. You'll just make it worse.'' He needed to get out and cool down.

Tony turned and left through the back door.

Julie stared after him, stifling a groan. Could she have made a bigger mess of things?

She didn't think so.

What she had wanted to say had come out all wrong. And Tony had been so...resistant.

Julie stood up and gathered the plates, carrying them to the sink.

Maybe he'd tried college and hadn't been successful. She hadn't missed how he avoided reading directions and making calculations. Maybe he had a learning problem, a disability. She should have thought things through before she brought the subject up.

She used her good arm to wash and rinse the dishes. She

didn't mean to make it sound like she thought his life wasn't worthwhile. She didn't understand why he would want to live in the middle of nowhere, but she didn't want him to think she was looking down at what he did.

Julie stared at the back door and wondered when Tony would return. She would have to apologize for butting in where she didn't belong.

He didn't come back that afternoon, or the next day. She kept busy, cleaning and patching nail holes and sanding the steps. Julie didn't know what else to do. His tools were still here, and as far as she was concerned he was still working for her. She'd call him, but he didn't even have a telephone.

How could you live in the middle of nowhere without a phone?

How had he gotten home? Was his truck repaired? She'd been doing nothing for two days except thinking about Tony. It would've been easy enough to walk around town and ask a few well-placed questions. She could have all the information she wanted. But the cost would be that everyone in Ferndale would know she was checking up on Tony. She wasn't willing to do that.

Julie finished cleaning out the kitchen cupboards and hauled the last of the stuff she was going to take back to L.A. out to the shed. She would start to paint tomorrow. When she closed the shed door and looked up across the yard, Tony was standing on the back steps watching her.

Relief flooded through her. She straightened and headed toward him. She'd been rehearsing this apology for two days.

She couldn't read his expression. What if he had just come back to get his belongings?

She had to make things right, she thought, launching into an apology. "Tony, I'm sorry if I offended you. I didn't mean to."

He nodded and motioned her into the house. "I know

that. I have some things to tell you. I shouldn't have left without letting you know when I'd be back."

He didn't sound angry. She followed him across the porch and into the kitchen. "Did you go home?"

He nodded. "Yeah, I got some work done on my place."

She took note of the scrapes and gouges on his hands. It looked like he had been battling some rough enemy. "Your truck?"

"Repaired." He gave her a wry smile. "We'll see how long it lasts."

"That's good." The silence hung there between them like a living thing.

Finally Tony spoke. "Do you want me to get my things and go?"

His words took Julie by surprise. "You mean not work for me anymore?" Did he think she would fire him over something that was her fault?

Tony nodded.

She had to tread very carefully. "Is that what you want?"

He shook his head. "No. But I will if you're not comfortable with me here."

"Tony, this was my fault. I butted in where I had no right. I want you to stay and finish. I want you to feel free to stay in the spare room when you're working here." She'd missed him.

Julie thought Tony looked relieved. "If you're okay with it, that would be good for me."

Julie was surprised at the rush of relief she felt. "I'm okay with it."

He studied her for a moment. "What have you been working on?"

She laughed. "You've heard of the very slow one-handed paper hanger? I'm the one-handed painter."

He reached out and traced his finger gently across her shoulder. "How's the collarbone?"

She almost shivered at his light touch. "Oh, it lets me know when I'm overdoing things."

"How about the stitches?" He caught her hand and pushed her sleeve up past her elbow.

She glanced down as he ran his thumb alongside the row of stitches, causing a tremor that shot up her arm.

He nodded. "Looks good. I can take them out for you tomorrow or the next day, if you want."

"You know how to do that?"

"Sure. Much easier than putting them in. Won't hurt a bit."

Tony shifted uncomfortably, let go of her arm and was quiet for a long time. Then he looked her in the eye. "I do have an education. I have an engineering degree."

Julie was so dumbfounded by Tony's announcement she didn't know what to say. She'd assumed he'd finished high school and joined the Navy.

"I didn't know."

"Yeah, I got that impression," he said in a dry tone. "I went to Annapolis. I didn't want my folks to go into debt to send me to college."

"Annapolis. Wow."

Tony nodded. "No one thought I'd make it because of the discipline. As a teenager, I was a little wild."

Now why didn't that surprise her? She remembered how fast he liked to drive.

"But once I got past the first semester, I found I kind of liked the way they ran things."

"Tight ship?" Julie smiled, loving the fact that he was confiding in her.

Tony rolled his eyes and grinned. "Oh, yeah, you could say that."

"So you chose engineering." There was so much she

wanted to ask, but would not. If he had things to tell her he would. She was trying so hard not to make any more mistakes.

"Yeah. Because of the way things are at Annapolis, with the required classes, most everyone ends up with an engineering degree. I couldn't come up with a better plan, so I went that route."

"And after school?"

"When you finish with the academy, you owe Uncle Sam payback. At first I was bored to tears, then I was accepted to SEAL training and found my niche."

"Liked the excitement, did you?" She thought about the way he reveled in speed and how restless he was if he wasn't busy.

He shrugged and looked a little sheepish. "I have to admit, I liked the excitement."

She laughed. An understatement for sure.

His face became very still and serious. "I think I mentioned I had an accident."

She nodded. This was sacred ground and she didn't want to repeat her mistake of two days ago, so she waited for him to say more.

Tony was silent for a long time. "I didn't know what happened. I don't remember anything, not only of the accident, but for a few days before and for two months after."

"Two months?" What was it like to lose two months of your life? She couldn't imagine.

"Yeah. I had to read the official report to find out."

After another long silence she prompted him in a gentle voice. "Will you tell me what you found out?"

He got that far away look she'd seen before. "We were on a mission, planting explosives. Something went wrong. Jimmy was killed and I had a fractured skull."

Oh, golly, Julie thought. That was so much worse than anything she had imagined. "Were you and Jimmy close?"

"Like brothers." There was a hitch in his voice he tried to cover by clearing his throat.

She chose her words very carefully. "Did the report tell you what you needed to know?"

"Not really. No one else had been close enough to see what happened." Anger erupted in his voice.

"Did the Navy investigate?" He seemed to need to talk, but she could tell it was costing him.

"They always do. But the explosion obliterated any physical evidence." He sounded disgusted.

She couldn't tell if it was because of the Navy or the circumstances.

"So, after you got better, you decided to leave the Navy." She gently prompted him.

He gave a short, bitter bark of laughter. "Oh, no. That decision was made for me."

"What do you mean?" Who would've made that serious a decision for him?

He rubbed the back of his head in an unconscious gesture. "Because of my head injury I couldn't dive anymore, so I was discharged."

"There wasn't a job you could do that didn't involve diving?" After all the time they must have spent training him, that didn't sound practical.

"You mean be stuck behind a desk? I didn't even consider it."

Julie understood. She couldn't picture Tony at a desk job, either. "So you came to Ferndale and bought property."

Tony stared at her for a moment. "The property I own now belonged to Jimmy. He'd inherited it from an uncle. He left it to me in his will because he didn't have any family."

Julie could see the hurt and confusion over his friend's death in his face. "That was hard, wasn't it?"

Tony moved so fast she didn't realize what he was doing until he pulled her up against his body and his mouth settled over hers. This was no gentle brushing of lips, but a full-on open mouth orgy of sensation. He kissed her until her knees were weak and she'd forgotten what they had been talking about.

Tony pulled back and stared at her. She blinked up at him, trying to get her bearings. "What...why..."

Tony nodded as if he understood her utter confusion and cleared his throat as he let go of her. "I think I'll get started on the closet door and windows in your room."

She watched him walk out of the kitchen. How could he do that? Kiss her until she couldn't see straight and then go on as if nothing had happened?

"Okay," she said to his retreating back. With the way her insides were quaking, she thought she might register on the Richter scale.

As he walked away she realized he'd done it again. Just as they had gotten to a difficult part of the conversation for him, he distracted her with a kiss.

The man certainly had an interesting technique for ending a conversation, and she found she liked it far more than she should, since he was only supposed to be a friend.

Chapter Eight

Julie sat cross-legged on the kitchen floor painting the cabinet under the sink and thinking about what had happened when Tony had returned.

She dipped her brush in the can of paint and applied the brush to the framing. She wasn't at all sure she liked the way Tony could knock her socks off with a kiss and then just walk away as if nothing had happened.

She could hear him hammering upstairs. He'd been working all afternoon, the noise from his work drifting down to her.

He used his kiss as a devastating weapon to shut her up. She dipped her brush back in the paint. Why couldn't he just tell her he didn't want to talk about something?

"How's it going?"

Julie flinched at the sound of his voice right behind her and splattered paint all over herself.

"How *do* you do that?"

"Do what?" he asked, grinning at the mess she'd made.

"Sneak up on me without making a noise?"

"I wasn't sneaking. You were concentrating so hard you didn't hear me." He pulled a rag out of his back pocket and took a swipe at her chin.

She jerked back and scowled at him.

"What? You have paint on your face," he said, all innocence.

"Just don't—" What was she going to say? Don't distract her? He did that by walking in a room. He did that by walking through her thoughts.

"Don't what?"

"Nothing," she muttered and dipped the brush again.

"I think painting is making you cranky."

"I'm not cranky. You make me sound like a child that needs a nap."

Tony waggled his eyebrows. "Want me to put you down for a nap?"

Julie felt the heat rise in her cheeks. "Tony, go away."

He held out his hand. "Come with me."

"Where?"

"A walk. Or better yet, a swim. We can go down to the beach. We need a break."

A break sounded heavenly. She was mighty tired of painting. "I wanted to get these cabinets finished."

He pulled the brush out of her hand and dropped it in a Ziploc bag. "Don't worry. The woodwork will be here when we get back. I'm almost finished upstairs and then I'll help you paint."

Julie ignored his outstretched hand and struggled to her feet.

The less she touched him the better.

"Okay. A short break." Then she would finish the painting herself. That was something she could do alone and save Tony for the jobs she couldn't handle. Besides, they would do better to stay in different parts of the house. She had a hard time concentrating when he was too close.

"Go put on a bathing suit and meet me down here."

"How about you?" She glanced down at his jeans.

Hands on her shoulders, he turned her toward the stairs. "Already put my suit on."

She stepped away from his touch and looked back over her shoulder at him. "Pretty sure of yourself, aren't you?"

"Yup." He grinned.

Julie left the room with her heart pounding. It wasn't fair that he had that effect on her.

She went upstairs and struggled into a one-piece bathing suit, then covered up with a long T-shirt.

By the time she got back down to the kitchen, Tony had assembled towels, two water bottles and a sack of sandwiches.

"You're pretty fast."

"You learn to be. We had to go wheels up on short notice."

"Wheels up?"

"Yeah, you know—ready for a mission and on the plane. Wheels up refers to the landing gear."

He picked up the bundle and they walked out to his truck. "We'll take the beast." He gestured to the old pickup. "I've got four-wheel drive and we can go out on the dunes."

"Okay." It felt so good to be getting out of the house she didn't really care where they went. She hadn't realized how cooped up she'd been feeling.

He drove down to the dunes and parked on the beach a safe distance from the surf.

"Want to swim?"

It had been an age since she'd been in the ocean. "Not really." The power of the surf intimidated her.

"Come on. I'll help you get past the breakers. Might be a little tough getting through the waves with that broken wing."

"I don't think..." She eyed the crashing waves.

"Come on. No chickening out. It'll be fun."

She didn't want him to think she was chicken. "Okay."

Julie eased her shirt off over her bad side and tossed it in the truck. She turned to see Tony staring at her.

She glanced down at her bathing suit. "What's the matter?"

"Nothing. Everything is perfect." He eyed her up and down.

She felt her face heating up. "Well, thanks," she said, wishing his approval didn't make her feel quite so good.

"Anytime," came the muffled reply as he peeled off his own shirt and started on the buttons of his fly.

Julie tore her gaze away and headed for the waves. She needed to get in the chilly water and cool off.

Tony caught up to her halfway to the water and then broke into a sprint and passed her.

Her steps slowed as she watched him speed up and dive into a braking wave. The sheer perfection of his honed body in a short pair of swim trunks took her breath away.

She had seen him without his shirt on, but the whole package was so much better than she could have imagined. With his slim hips, muscled legs, wide shoulders and taut, brawny arms, he looked like a poster boy for physical fitness.

He swam out about fifty yards and then back through the breaking surf, catching a wave and riding it in to where she stood in the surf line, water lapping around her ankles.

He made body surfing look effortless. She knew better.

He smoothed his wet hair back from his face. "Ready to get wet?"

"I guess." She walked in a few feet and shuddered as a wave broke against her legs. Even at the peak of the summer the ocean here never really got warm.

She took a step back.

Tony made a grab for her arm. "Come on, get in. You'll get used to it quick enough."

He held on to her and braced her against a breaking wave, turning her so that he took the brunt of the force. The temperature of the water rising up her torso took her breath away.

"Wait! It's too cold!"

He made a clucking noise like a chicken and kept guiding her further and further out until they made it past the breaking surf.

He had an annoying habit of pushing her into things she wasn't sure she wanted, she grumbled to herself even as she admitted she was becoming accustomed to the cold water.

This far out the turbulence was gone and the ocean moved them up and down with gentle swells.

She was very aware of his body plastered up against her back.

He kept his arm around her waist. "You doing okay?"

Julie nodded. "You can let me go." She was starting to warm up and it had nothing to do with the temperature of the water.

He drew his hand away slowly. It felt like a lover's caress.

"I'm going to swim a little, then I'll come back. Don't worry if you drift. I'll find you."

He set out and within moments his strong stroke had carried him so far out his dark head reminded her of a seal bobbing in the water.

Julie turned onto her back and let the sun warm her face as she floated in the buoyant saltwater, loving the feel of the swells and current against her body. She hadn't expected to feel such a sense of serenity. The vastness of the ocean should have been unsettling, but she found it soothing.

Her thoughts drifted to Tony and the relief she'd felt when she'd seen him standing on her porch this morning. She had to admit it was more than completing the work on the house.

She'd missed him.

She didn't want to feel the way she did. He lived in Ferndale, building a life that she wanted no part of.

She wanted to get back to L.A., to the hum and energy of the city. She could lose herself in L.A.

In Ferndale it was too quiet. There was too much time to think, and the ghosts from her past kept sneaking up on her.

As a large swell rocked her gently she remembered what it had been like here when she arrived at Bessie's house after her parents' deaths. How alone she had been. She'd had family and lots of friends in L.A. In Ferndale she'd had nothing.

Tony arrived and she gladly abandoned her depressing thoughts. He shook the water out of his hair like a dog and asked, "Ready to head in?"

She would have liked to stay longer, she realized with surprise, but there was still a great deal of work to finish today. "Ready."

"I'll take you through the surf. You just relax and let me do the work."

When she nodded he turned her towards the shore and hooked an arm around her waist. The feel of his wet warm body up against hers was heavenly.

He gave her a little shake. "Loosen up. You're fighting me."

How did he expect her to relax while he had her plastered up against his body?

She took a deep breath and tried to force her arms and legs to go limp. "Okay."

He turned his lips against her temple. "Come on, Julie. You trust me, don't you?"

She did trust him. This was the first time she'd ever really enjoyed swimming in the ocean. She just wasn't too sure she trusted herself.

He towed her into shore and let go of her when her feet could touch the sandy bottom. She was surprised when she walked out of the surf and her legs felt a little rubbery.

"How long were we out there?"

Tony squinted up at the sun. "Probably an hour."

It hadn't seemed nearly that long.

They sank down on their towels and she pulled her shirt on over her wet suit.

Tony flopped back on his towel, watching her. He wished she hadn't put her shirt on. He really liked looking at her. At least those long gorgeous legs of hers were still within his view.

"Hungry?" he asked.

She thought for a moment, then nodded. She did that all the time, he thought. Gave everything serious consideration, even something as simple as being hungry. He got the impression she was afraid of making mistakes, even little ones.

He dug out the sandwiches, handing her one along with a water bottle.

"When the house sells, are you going to use the money to buy something in L.A.?" He knew she was renting an apartment now. He hated the thought of her moving away from Ferndale.

She looked at him for a long time, as if she were making up her mind whether or not to answer him. "No. I'm going to quit my job and write."

From her hesitancy he figured this was something she hadn't shared with very many people. "Wow! That's great. What kind of writing do you do?"

Her look of relief at his response told him a lot. "Children's books. I want to write books for ten- to twelve-year-olds."

He shifted so he could grab another sandwich and still see the excited expression on her face. "What kinds of stories?"

"Adventure stories. Children that age love exciting literature."

"Have you started writing any yet?"

"Yes. I have one finished and the next two plotted." She sighed. "It's taken me two years to do that much. I want time off from teaching to get a really good proposal together before I submit."

He knew nothing about publishing. "That's important?"

"Yes, I think so. I want them to know I'm serious about a career."

Careful Julie would do just that, Tony mused as he bit into a second sandwich.

"May I ask you a question?" She had stopped eating.

"Sure," he said, wondering at the serious look on her face.

"Where are you getting the money to build your house?"

Oh, God. He tensed up. He hadn't seen this coming. "My buddy left me the land." *After I got him killed.* Tony tried to keep a pleasant look plastered on his face. "And I got his death benefits. Ninety thousand dollars."

Her eyes widened when he named the amount. "And he left everything to you?"

"Yes. Except for ten thousand."

She looked confused. "Who got the ten thousand?"

Tony smiled. "The platoon."

"For what? Did you have a widows' and orphans' fund?"

Tony shook his head. "No. The single guys usually designate ten thousand to go to a party."

A look of disbelief crossed her face. "You mean like a wake?"

He considered her question. "Yeah, I guess you could call it that."

"Must have been one heck of a party."

He'd still been in the hospital and had missed it, but Jimmy's send-off had become a legend among the SEAL teams. "Yup. One heck of a party." Good thing he'd missed it. He wouldn't have been able to celebrate.

He still had half the sandwich in his hand when she brushed the sand off those wonderful legs of hers and stood up. "We need to get back. I have a lot I want to finish today."

Happy to end the conversation, Tony got up and followed her back to the parking lot.

He turned his thoughts away from Jimmy and back to Julie. He wanted to give her a fair day's work for his pay, but the idea of her leaving was making him miserable. Every day of work brought him a day closer to Julie leaving.

He wondered if L.A. was as lousy a place as he imagined.

Julie watched Tony shift his weight on the ladder to steady himself, then rip another piece of the ugly paneling off the dining room wall, handing it down to her.

She carried it across the room and added it to the growing stack. "How do you know you don't like cities if you've never lived in one?"

Tony wiped his forehead on the shoulder of his T-shirt. "I've never lived in a rat hole but I know I wouldn't like it."

Hands on her hip, she gave him a sour look. "Harsh, Tony, harsh."

He shrugged. Every time he did that she wanted to drool over those wide shoulders.

"Yeah, well, all the things I like best are in the country."

"Like?" Her chin jutted out in a belligerent pose.

"Clean air."

She had to admit there was a definite shortage of that in L.A. "And?"

"No traffic jams."

Well, she had to admit he had her there, too. Before she could say more he said, "Wide-open spaces. To run and to ride. Horses. Can you keep one in your apartment?"

"Okay, you're telling me all the negatives. But there are plenty of positives to balance them out."

"Like?"

He mimicked her belligerent pose and she stifled a smile.

"Theater. Movies. Plays. Concerts."

He ripped off another strip of paneling. "Ferndale does have a shortage there. Do you go a lot? To the theater?"

She took the wood from him and added it to the pile. She hadn't been to a live performance in over two years, but she didn't want to admit it to him.

"It's important to me." She just liked knowing she could go if she wanted.

"What else?" He used a clawhammer to pry a stubborn piece loose.

She thought for a moment. "Restaurants."

He grinned at her. "Yeah, I guess that would be important to someone who can't cook. Why, you could starve to death in Ferndale."

He thought he was so cute. "I can cook. I just don't think it's worth the time it takes."

She'd have to eat in when she wasn't working. Her budget would need a major restructure when she quit work.

He was laughing. "I'm not sure peanut butter and jelly qualifies as cooking."

She held out her hand for another strip of paneling. "Stop trying to change the subject."

As soon as she said it she was reminded of how he kissed her silly when he didn't want to talk about something. She was tempted to steer the conversation to one of his off-limits topics.

Instead she said, "Friends."

Tony shook his head. "I have friends in Ferndale."

"I mean lots of friends. You have to admit the pool here is pretty small."

He became still and quiet as he studied her. "Maybe you're too selective."

She bristled at his remark. "Are you calling me a snob?"

He shook his head. "No. But there is a difference between quantity and quality."

He was judging her friends and he'd never even met them. "You think your friends here are better than mine?"

He put up a gloved hand. "Whoa. I didn't mean the quality of the person, I meant of the friendship."

She still felt slightly insulted. "What do you mean?"

He paused, as if he were choosing his words very carefully. "How many of your vast number of friends have come to Ferndale or called to offer to help you with the house?"

It had never occurred to her that anyone would want to come all the way up here just to help. Most of them didn't have the skills, anyway. "Well none, but—"

"And how many have called to see how you were doing?"

None. But then, most didn't even know she had left town. Because she hadn't been close enough to most of them to bother to tell them her plans. They were the kind of friends you ran in to at parties, not the kind that shared your day-to-day plans.

Julie pushed the thought aside. She wasn't the type of person who had close friends she would bare her soul to. Like old underwear, her soul had too many snags and flaws to be showing it to other people.

She decided they had talked enough on that subject. She changed direction. "I bet if you gave the city a try you'd like it better than you think."

"Doubtful."

"But not impossible. Or are you afraid to be wrong?"

"No. When I'm wrong I can admit it." A flash of pain crossed Tony's face. Silently he climbed down and moved the ladder over a few feet.

Julie wanted to reach out to him. Why had her comment caused his reaction? They worked for a few minutes without talking.

Julie wished she had brought the radio downstairs from her bedroom. The quiet bothered her.

"Why did your grandmother put paneling over the windows?" They had worked their way around two walls of the dining room, uncovering windows that let in bright sunlight.

He ripped another strip off and handed it to her. "She did it before I came to live with her. She told me she had it put up when the heathens moved in next door."

One eyebrow went up. "The heathens?"

Julie laughed. "That's what she called them. They were nudists and apparently they never closed their drapes."

Tony leaned away from the ladder and ducked his head so he could see out the window. "Deliver us from temptation."

Julie laughed. "Down boy. They moved out years ago."

"And she didn't bother to take the paneling down after they left?"

"Bessie was never big on change. Once she did something, it stayed that way."

"Well, it'll look a hundred times better without it." He ran his hand over the smooth plaster wall. "The woodwork is in good shape. I'll patch the nail holes in the plaster and you can decide if you want to paint."

"Okay." He was right. The improvement was terrific. The house would show a lot better with this room redone.

His voice pulled her away from her thoughts. "Your stitches can come out today. Do you want me to do it, or do you want to go back to the doctor?"

She didn't want to face a lengthy wait in the doctor's office or the paperwork she would have to fill out for her insurance company. She glanced down at the little threads.

She gave him a long look, considering her options. "You really know how to do it?"

"Sure. I've had stitches a few times. It's a lot easier than getting a cast off."

"You've done that, too? Taken off a cast?" Somehow she wasn't surprised.

He nodded as he climbed off the ladder. "I broke my arm three times as a kid. Every summer for three years running."

She tried not to look at the way his jeans pulled across his butt as he backed down the steps. "And did you always remove your own cast?"

His feet hit the floor and he turned toward her. "Just the second and third time. It was hot and I wanted to go swimming."

Removing your own cast hardly sounded like a good idea. "What about the broken bone?"

He flexed his arm in an unconscious gesture and his biceps strained against the soft white cotton of his shirt. "Well, they tell you you need to wear the cast for six weeks, but the bone is pretty well mended after a month."

She swallowed, trying to work up saliva in her suddenly dry mouth. "How do you get a cast off?"

"Plaster is easy. Garden pruners. Fiberglass is a little tougher."

She tried to picture him as a child. "What did you use for fiberglass?"

He thought for a moment. "Garden pruners and a little patience."

Patience. Right. She laughed. "Which you seemed to be short of."

He shrugged. "I was a kid."

Some how she didn't think he'd changed all that much. He didn't appear to have patience when it came to anything that slowed him down physically.

Hesitantly she asked, "What do you need for taking out the stitches?" Despite her misgivings, she'd let him do one.

"Do you have a pair of little scissors? And tweezers?"

Bessie had done a lot of sewing and needlework. Her basket was still in the living room. "Let me go look."

Julie found a pair of scissors shaped like a bird with tiny curved blades where the beak would be. She went upstairs and got tweezers from her makeup kit.

She came back to the dining room and held them up. "Will these do?"

"Perfect. Come into the kitchen."

Tony went to the sink and washed his hands, then he positioned two kitchen chairs side by side, facing opposite directions.

He guided her into one of the chairs and sat in the other, so close their thighs were touching. He took hold of her arm and studied the stitches. "Looks good. Ready?"

The warmth from his body reassured her. He brought his knee up, hooking one foot on the rung of the chair. Grasping her wrist, he laid her arm across his knee. She was acutely aware of the firm muscle and heated skin under her forearm.

Julie took a deep breath and closed her eyes, remembering how it had felt to have the gash stitched up. "Ready."

She braced herself as she felt him run his finger over the line of stitches, determined not to flinch and make the situation worse. She counted to ten and concentrated on her breathing, wondering when he was going to start. The wait was making her crazy.

Avoiding looking down at her arm, she turned her head to look at him, and asked him to hurry up.

Tony smiled and leaned toward her. "Okay."

She stared at his mouth. She really liked his mouth. It distracted her from what he was about to do. "I'm ready."

"No. Okay, you're done."

She looked down at her elbow and all the little black threads were gone.

"How did you do that?" She ran her finger over the scar. She hadn't felt a thing.

He still had a hold of her arm and he was running his thumb just behind hers over the bright pink line. "It's a lot easier taking them out than putting them in."

She became very aware of the feel of his hand on her arm and the warmth of his body next to hers. She wanted to lean into him and see where the situation would take them.

Apparently Tony was thinking the same thing as his eyes fastened on her lips and he pulled her gently toward him.

Just as his lips were about to settle on hers, the loud grinding ring of the doorbell cut into their moment.

He muttered something under his breath and let go of her arm.

After he left the kitchen, Julie put her hand over her pounding heart, wondering where they might have ended up if they hadn't been interrupted.

Julie fanned herself with her hand. She could hear Tony talking to someone at the front door.

She got up and scooped the little pile of silk threads that had held her cut together into her hand and dumped them into the trash. She picked up the scissors and tweezers. Tony came back into the kitchen as she was pushing the chairs underneath the table where they belonged.

He stopped in the doorway and studied her long enough to make her uncomfortable.

"Who was at the door?"

"The kid who works at Valley Grocery as a box boy. He was wondering if you wanted help clearing out the yard."

She'd love help with the outdoor work, but she certainly didn't have the money in her budget for hiring anyone else.

"Did you tell him no?"

"I told him doubtful."

"Good. I plan to handle that myself. The collarbone is getting better each day." She raised her arm as high as she could without pain to show Tony her progress.

"Well don't push it. You don't want to reinjure yourself."

She was a little surprised at him. He pushed himself to the limit whenever he could.

He studied her for a long moment, but she couldn't read his expression. "Shall we get back to work?"

"Sure." Julie said brightly. What she really wanted to get back to was what they had been doing when the doorbell rang and interrupted them. She was absolutely sure it would be a lot more fun than stripping paneling.

Chapter Nine

Tony worked on the roof of his house and tried not to think about Julie, which was impossible because he thought about her all the time. The way she looked, the way she smelled.

He wanted her.

Day and night, she haunted his thoughts.

According to her, they had little in common. Julie wanted to believe that everything he liked she hated. He was starting to wonder. Was it really small town living that she detested, or was she hiding out in the big city?

He needed to talk to Betty when she returned. She'd been a friend of Julie's grandmother and could tell him what it had been like for Julie when she came to Ferndale. It couldn't have been easy, losing her parents at such a young age and then being sent to live with a grandmother she wasn't close to.

He didn't particularly like the idea of going to Betty, but Julie wasn't going to tell him anything. She'd brushed him off whenever he tried to talk about her time in Ferndale.

Hadn't he bared his soul to her? Told her things about the accident and Jimmy's death he'd never told anyone?

Tony nailed another shingle onto his roof. He needed to figure this situation out because...

Because he was in love with her.

Just like that, his arm raised and his hammer in mid-swing, it hit him.

He loved Julie.

Tony slammed his hammer down on the head of the nail then tipped his face up to the sky.

"Why her?" he shouted.

Why would he be so stupid to fall in love with a girl who seemed to like breathing smog and living on concrete?

Because she was the most wonderful woman that had ever walked into his life.

He whacked another nail home and tried to talk himself out of loving her.

Maybe he was mistaken and it was just the proximity. Living with a gorgeous woman and not sharing a bed could drive a man to the edge of frustration. Maybe he was just mistaking lust for love.

He tried to picture other women he'd dated seriously and couldn't come up with a mental picture of a single one of them. The thought of Julie selling the house in Ferndale and going back to L.A. made his gut ache in a way it never had before.

He slammed his hammer down on another nail and felt cold sweat trickle down his back. He'd been consumed with building his house before he met her and now he had to tear himself away from her to work on it. Right now he was counting the hours until he could drive back to Ferndale.

He knew she was attracted to him, but if she had to choose between him and L.A. he didn't like his odds.

He finished the last row of shingles and slid down to where the ladder rested against the side of his house.

He needed a plan, a way to keep Julie in Ferndale. She had her dream to write. She could do that anywhere. He had to convince her that small towns weren't bad places to live.

He tossed his hammer into the toolbox. Maybe he should start by showing her what he was building. And telling her why it was so important to him. He knew she thought he should have a career. He hadn't forgotten what she had said about getting an education and a real job.

He stood staring at his house. He wanted her to give up her life in L.A. for him.

Would he be willing to give this up for her?

He wasn't sure.

As he lowered the extension ladder and carried it into the house he realized he'd told her as much as he knew of the accident, but he hadn't told her what it had done to him to lose Jimmy. And not be a SEAL anymore. To lose his identity and his best friend and not know why.

Maybe it was time he told her. He had to be honest with her, even though she might not even like him after he spilled his guts.

She'd offered to help him with his reading. He'd take her up on that. It was a way to spend more time with her. His reading was still halting at best. After the accident he'd taken a class for people with brain injuries, but he had become impatient and quit so he could move here to Ferndale.

He stripped off his clothes and stepped under the solar shower. He needed a plan. A strategy. He was going to treat Julie like a mission.

He would set his agenda, gather his weapons and zero in on his target. If SEAL training had taught him anything, it had shown him the necessity of a well-executed plan.

When he pulled up in front of her house, Julie was on the front porch wearing shorts and her old paint-stained shirt, finishing up a coat of primer on the new wood.

She was the most beautiful woman he had ever known.

She looked up, rocked back on her heels and gave him a smile of welcome that warmed him through and through. Her long, tanned legs drew his attention.

He swung his gaze down to what she was doing. "Hey. Looks good." He climbed down from the cab and went around to the bed of his truck and pulled out the base of his table saw.

"What are you going to do?"

"Replace the boards with dry rot under the sink upstairs."

Julie made a face. "Necessary?"

"You'll have to do it or disclose it to your buyer. One less thing to haggle over price-wise."

He saw her sigh as he lugged the equipment up the front walk.

"I know." He glanced at her loose shirt and wondered if she was wearing anything underneath. "But the higher price you get for the property will more than cover what I'm making. And you'll sell faster, too."

He didn't like the way she brightened at that. He'd just admitted to himself how much he wanted her to stay in Ferndale.

He couldn't resist the dig. "Yup, the quicker I fix things up the quicker you can get back to the smog and traffic of L.A."

She threw a paint-stained rag at him.

It fell short by half. He watched the downward arch of the flimsy projectile. "You throw like a girl."

She stared at him for a moment. "What's the matter with you today? How come you're in such a sour mood?"

Because I just discovered I love you and this isn't going

to have a good ending, he wanted to say. Instead he shrugged and hauled more equipment out of the truck bed.

"I'll set this up in the backyard if that's okay."

"Wouldn't it be better to be closer to where you're working?"

He brought the rag back to her and stood on the only unpainted board on the steps. "It makes a heck of a mess. You don't want that inside."

Julie pushed herself to her feet. "Have you had lunch?"

He'd been so anxious to see her he'd forgotten to eat. Bad sign. "Nope. What are you offering?" Her best seemed to be peanut butter and jelly.

"I walked to the market today and picked up some groceries. How about a roast beef sandwich?"

Tony grinned. "How about two? You want me to make them?"

"No. I'll manage. You get set up." She wiped her hands on the rag and went in the house through the front door.

He watched her until he couldn't see her anymore. Then he carried his equipment through the side gate into the yard, found a level spot under the clothesline and set up the saw. Every trip he made back to his truck he glanced in through the back porch and watched Julie standing at the counter assembling the sandwiches.

When he was finished hauling his stuff he went in through the back door. She was setting plates on the table.

He decided to quit taking the fact that he loved her out on her. "That looks great." She had a smear of paint under her chin.

She smiled at him. "You're easy to please."

"Not really," he muttered under his breath.

"What?" She looked up, puzzled.

He shook his head. "Nothing."

They slid into their seats and ate silently for a while.

After he had polished off one of the sandwiches, he decided the timing was right to talk.

"Julie?"

She looked up. "Yes?" His expression must have alarmed her because her smile faded.

He hesitated for a moment, reaching for courage. Asking for help was so hard for him. "Remember when you offered to help me with my reading?"

"Of course."

He hesitated. "Are you still willing?"

A look of relief passed over her face. "Yes. I'll help you as much as I can. Anytime."

Her smile reassured him. "This afternoon? After we finish work?"

"Sure. All you have to do is cook dinner." She jerked her thumb toward the refrigerator.

He liked the way she asked for an exchange of favors. It made him feel better.

She always made him feel better.

"Deal." He extended his hand across the table.

She slid her palm against his and his fingers curled around her warm, slender hand. It fit perfectly in his.

Julie scanned the built-in bookcase in the living room. It didn't look like Bessie had gotten any new books in the last ten years. She had no idea how much of a problem Tony had, but she could tell it had been hard for him to ask for help. She would have to be very careful of his ego.

She chose three books of varying difficulty, one a *Reader's Digest* volume with larger print, one gothic romance, and the Penelope Fitzgerald novel *The Beginning of Spring* she had given Bessie for Christmas one year. The book's spine was so stiff she was sure her grandmother had never opened it.

If she was able to give Tony any help at all she would

have to go to the library and get some books that would hold his interest. This selection wasn't going to do it.

She stared at the short stack of books in her arms and went over the points she had learned in a workshop last year on screening children who were having difficulty with reading. The hard part would be pinpointing his actual problem.

Julie set the books on the table in the dining room and wandered into the kitchen. Tony stood at the counter chopping ingredients for a salad. She could smell the chicken she had bought this morning cooking in the oven, and there was a pot of water boiling on the stove.

She'd trade her expertise as a teacher for a home-cooked meal any day of the week. "Smells great. When do we eat?"

He glanced at her over his shoulder. "About a half hour."

"Great. I have time for a shower."

Tony nodded and said, "Don't run any water in the sink," then turned back to what he was doing.

As Julie started up the stairs she realized what a comfortable routine they had fallen into. Her steps slowed. They worked well together, anticipating each other's needs. She looked forward to him being here.

She'd miss him when she left.

She stopped about halfway up the stairs, shaking off a sudden feeling of melancholy. Of course she'd miss him.

They had become friends.

But nothing more. She didn't *want* anything more.

She started up the stairs again. She wouldn't let it be anything more.

She went in her room and grabbed some clean clothes. After closing the bathroom door she stripped off her shorts and eased out of her shirt.

It was too dangerous to get too close to someone else. To need them in your life.

To love them.

Because when you loved them and they left the hurt was so bad you never recovered from it.

So she and Tony would be friends. And when she went home he would stay here and they would have their separate lives and both of them would be fine.

Because she wasn't going to love him. Or anyone. Ever.

She stepped under the spray and felt much better now that she had had that little talk with herself.

Julie listened to Tony tell her what the doctors had told him to expect after the accident. Then she had him read until he began to falter and a note of frustration crept into his voice.

She put her hand on his arm. "That's enough."

He looked up from the book. "I can do more."

"You mean push yourself?"

"Yeah."

"I suspect you always push yourself, no matter what you're doing."

He frowned and thought for a minute. "Mostly, yes."

She slid the book out of his hands. "Well I don't think that's a good idea now. You're starting to get frustrated." She watched him squint a little when he looked at her, his expression unreadable.

She remembered an article she had read on head injuries. "You have a headache, too, don't you?"

He paused for a moment, then nodded. "Yes."

"Do you always get one when you read?"

"If I read long enough." He shrugged.

She leaned to the side so she could look directly at his face. "I don't think your eyes are tracking properly."

"They're better than they used to be."

Old news to him, she thought. But he had failed to mention it. She wondered what else he hadn't told her. "That's good news."

"I suppose." He sounded angry.

Sympathy for this man of action overwhelmed her. She laid a hand on his arm. "But you want it to be perfect, right?"

He sighed. "Yes."

Head injuries were so unpredictable. "It may never be. Can you live with that?"

"Do I have a choice?" he growled.

"No. When things happen you don't have a choice." She thought about her parents' deaths.

He jerked his chair back and stood up. "It pisses me off."

"I know. You need to be in control and this is out of your control."

Tony rubbed at his temples then stared down at her for a long moment. "It seems like not much has been in my control for a long time."

Julie decided to go out on a limb and ask about his accident. It might do him a lot of good to talk about it. "Will you tell me what happened?"

Tony shrugged and was silent for so long she thought he wasn't going to talk. Then he sat down and leaned forward, folding his arms on the table. He stared at the wall in front of him as he spoke.

"We were in South America. Jimmy and I were part of an advance team doing drug interdiction. We were setting up explosives and something went wrong."

"Do you know what?" she urged him gently.

He shook his head and continued to stare at the wall. "I've tried to remember every day since I woke up in the hospital in San Diego. I don't even remember the day before the accident. I don't remember the mission or leaving the States.''

''How about the others that were there?''

''They were pretty far away. They knew what we were doing. But not what caused the explosion.'' His voice was full of pain.

Her heart went out to him. ''You think it was your fault, don't you?''

''Jimmy was an expert at explosives,'' he said, shaking his head.

She was beginning to understand. At first she'd thought he blamed Jimmy for the accident. ''So you assume it must have been your fault?''

''Yeah. Pretty much.'' He nodded, misery plain in his expression.

Gently she prompted him. ''If Jimmy was the expert, wouldn't he have been in charge of what you were doing?''

He slammed his fist down on the tabletop. ''Yeah, but I must have screwed up.''

Her heart ached for him. ''That's a pretty huge assumption.''

He glared at her. ''Well, I'm here and he's dead. That pretty much tells the story, doesn't it?''

She rubbed her hand along his arm, then took his clenched fist between her two hands. ''This unknown situation seems a whole lot clearer to you than it does to me.''

He stared at her, but he didn't pull away.

She squeezed his hand. ''I know about survivor guilt. My parents were killed in a car accident when I was fourteen.''

He relaxed a fraction. ''Were you in the car?''

''No. They were on their way to pick me up from a friend's house. So it was my fault.''

''No, it wasn't.'' His voice was full of surprise. He

pulled a hand out of her grasp and stroked his thumb over her wrist.

"Not from where you stand. But it's what *I* thought for a long time. There's nothing reasonable about survivor's guilt. You just have it. And after a while, you learn to live with it. And if you're lucky, you learn to get past it."

"Did you?" He held both her hands now between his.

"What?" The warmth of his palms distracted her.

"Get past it?" He brought her hands to his lips and kissed them gently.

His gentle sympathy touched her. "Yes. Mostly. Holidays are hard. My birthday is the worst, because it brings back the memories of how special they made that day for me growing up."

Tony nodded and studied her face.

She stared back into his solemn gray eyes. "What days are going to be tough for you?"

"Every day I look out my windows at the land Jimmy left me. I remember it should have been him there and not me."

Her heart went out to him. "You know what helped?"

"No. What?"

"Learning to say thank you for each day instead of feeling like I didn't deserve it." She'd never shared her thoughts with anyone before, but she sensed a kindred spirit in Tony.

"How long did that take you?"

His voice sounded so hopeful she wanted to cry. "I'm still working on it." She felt the tears she had been holding back well up.

Tony reached over and pulled her to her feet, then settled her onto his lap, wrapping his arms around her.

She lay her head on his shoulder and let his strength surround her, feeling more comforted than she had since losing her parents more than ten years before.

She decided not to think too much about that.

* * *

Tony shifted his weight on the ladder to reach out with a putty knife filled with spackle and patched the last of the nail holes in the dining-room wall.

Julie knelt on a tarp across the room, applying paint to the wide baseboards. He paused and watched her work. Her ponytail hung over one shoulder, exposing her small pretty ears and the back of her neck.

He wanted to climb down off the ladder and put his lips on that smooth patch of skin.

Down boy, he thought. This was not the time to rush things.

If he told her how much she meant to him, he would scare her off, and that was the last thing he wanted to do. Since she had gotten him to talk about Jimmy he had felt himself start to heal, and he owed her for that precious gift. He'd thought it was impossible for him to come to terms with what had happened.

He slapped some more spackle on the wall, considering his dilemma. He needed to give her time to deal with her own demons.

Julie was so sure she didn't want to live in Ferndale he was going to have to go slow. Moving too fast with spooky horses was a bad idea, and he figured it was the same with a woman.

But there was precious little time left.

He scraped the excess spackle off the wall and looked around. He couldn't believe how different the room looked without the paneling. Bright sunshine flooded the room, making it feel airy and cheerful.

He chuckled over the memory of why Julie's grandmother had put up the paneling in the first place. Nudists in Ferndale. Now wasn't that an interesting thought? The town must have been appalled.

"What's so funny?" Julie's voice interrupted his thoughts.

"I was just thinking of the neighbors."

Julie laughed.

Tony loved the sound of her laugh.

"Can you imagine? I'm sure people were beside themselves. I don't think they lived there very long."

"I suppose not." He glanced out the window again. "It's a beautiful day. Want to take a drive?"

She smiled up at him. "Considering the price of gas, that's a generous offer."

He shrugged, as if he didn't care one way or the other. "You said you've never seen the Lost Coast. Want to go this afternoon?" He worked to make his offer sound casual. He felt as if his life might depend on her answer.

She raised an eyebrow and laid her brush on top of the open can of paint. "You want to take me to your land?"

She asked the question in such a neutral tone of voice he couldn't read her feelings.

"Yeah, we could stop by," he said, trying to match her tone.

She seemed to consider his offer far too long. Finally she said, "Okay. I'll be done here in a few minutes."

Tony simply nodded and turned back to the wall, then felt a huge grin splitting his face.

Tony pulled up beside his half-built house and helped Julie out of the truck, then watched her look around.

He tried to remember what it had been like for him to see this land for the first time. The rolling grassy hills, huge old oaks, soaring hawks and the Pacific Ocean glittering in the distance.

He searched her face and couldn't tell what she was thinking. He didn't want her reaction to be so important to him, but it was. He had the frightening feeling his future was hooked to how she would see it, and there was nothing he could do about it.

When she turned toward him, she smiled.

"What do you think?" he asked, trying to hide his eagerness.

Her eyes swept the land again and she cleared her throat. "It's so…empty." She laughed. "You can tell I'm not used to the wide-open spaces."

He tried to ignore the edge of uneasiness in her voice. His eyes made a sweep from north to south. "Yeah. It's great. I can't even see my neighbors."

"I noticed that," Julie murmured. "Show me the house."

Tony took her by the arm and guided her around the lumber piled on the deep west-facing porch. "I'll sit out here and watch the sun set."

And I want you by my side.

Julie nodded and turned to look at the view.

Her face told him nothing. She wore a pleasant expression and he couldn't read what was going on underneath. He wanted to shake her and tell her to look again so she would see how wonderful it was.

He took her arm again and urged her through the front door opening. "I know it looks a long way from finished, but the big stuff is done. I finished the roof last week, and the plumbing and electrical is installed. The windows will be here some time this week, then the siding and drywall goes up pretty quick."

He maneuvered her into the kitchen. Gesturing with his arm he indicated the east wall. "The cabinets and appliances will be along this wall, and the west wall will be a row of windows to take advantage of the view."

He pointed to the waist high area below the window openings. "This will all be sink and counter work space."

Julie nodded politely as he showed her around. "Did you do the design yourself?"

He smiled at her. "Yeah, with a lot of help from the Internet. I found a couple of sites that had plans I liked."

She looked around. "Do you have electricity?"

"No. I'm working off a generator until the county extends the lines. It's out back next to my trailer." He pointed toward the back of his house. The trailer where he had been living was visible through the studs.

"That's where you sleep?" She sounded as if she didn't believe him.

He eyed the rusty old trailer, realizing what it must look like to her. "Sure. It's only temporary. And a lot better than a lot of places I've slept." At least it was dry and relatively warm.

"What do you mean?"

"When I was a SEAL we'd often sleep out in the open. In all kinds of weather."

"You didn't have tents?"

Tony laughed. "When you're carrying over a hundred pounds of gear, you don't have room to haul a tent, too."

She looked appalled. "What about when it rained?"

He shrugged. "We got wet. And when it snowed, we dug a hole and slept in it." If they were lucky enough to stop and sleep.

She shook her head. "And you miss that?"

Tony laughed. "Not that. I miss the team, and the excitement."

She stared at him. "This is definitely one of those guy things."

He smiled. "Yeah. Pretty much." He remembered how he'd gone with several members of his team to see the movie with the female recruit going through SEAL training. They'd thought it was the best comedy they'd ever seen.

Her voice broke into his thoughts. "How long until you can move in?"

"I want to be in the house by October."

She glanced around again and raised an eyebrow. "You can do that and still work on my house?"

"I'll manage." Tony was putting in fourteen-hour days here on the days he didn't stay at Julie's. Even on the days he traveled back and forth to Ferndale he managed to get several hours of work done on his own house.

There wasn't much he could do now because he was waiting on a shipment of lumber so he could start on the siding.

"I'm impressed. This is a lot of work for one person."

"I have a buddy coming in about a month or so, as soon as he can get some time off. That will be a big help when it comes time to put up the siding."

They'd left the kitchen. Tony was following Julie as she wandered down the hallway leading to the bedrooms. She stopped and pointed to a series of capped pipes. "Bathroom?"

"Right. Sink, toilet and tub with shower."

She moved on ahead of him, then stopped again. "Bedroom?"

"These three rooms will all be bedrooms." He indicated the next three openings in the studs. "The living room is opposite the kitchen on the west wall."

"Lots of space."

Did he dare tell her when he laid it out he'd thought it was too much space?

Then he'd met her.

He could picture her here. She could have the west-facing bedroom for her office. A view like that would have to inspire creativity. She could write her books right here.

There was enough room for children. He'd never pictured wanting that with another woman.

He didn't say anything. It was way too soon to tell her he wanted to spend his life with her. But for the last few days he couldn't think of anything else.

He cleared his throat, feeling panicked that he couldn't tell what she thought of his place.

His happiness was hanging in the balance. "I need some things from my trailer. I'll get them now and put them in the truck."

Julie nodded. "I'll just wander around."

She watched Tony sprint towards the back of the house. The man never walked, she thought with a smile.

Julie walked back the way they had come and out onto the wide porch. He was amazing. The house was going to be really special. Even her untrained eye could see that.

She went down the steps and stood with the house at her back. She couldn't see a sign of civilization. No roads, no power lines or telephone poles. She scanned the sky. Perfect blue, cloudless and empty.

And quiet. There was not a sound except for a high-pitched whistle she assumed must be a bird.

It was so lonely she wanted to run back to where Tony was just to reassure herself she wasn't alone. How did people live like this? She hated the quiet. It gave too much opportunity for thoughts she didn't want to have.

It made her feel weak and small that she couldn't stand to be alone with just her thoughts to keep her company. She held her ground. Surely she could manage to withstand five minutes of silence. Her breathing had increased and her palms were sweaty by the time Tony found her out front.

She turned to find him studying her. It seemed so important to him that she like what he was building here.

She gave him a bright smile. "The house is amazing. You're amazing."

He looked surprised and pleased. "Thanks."

"No, I mean it. There aren't many people who could do what you're doing."

He let his gaze travel over the landscape and his expression softened. "It's not so hard."

He took her hand. "Let's take a walk. I'll show you where I'm going to put the barn and the corrals."

He talked as they walked, but she only half listened to his words, concentrating more on his tone and expression.

She knew he still suffered guilt over his friend's death, but he was coping. This property was his because his friend had died. How did he manage to make it his dream?

He said it wasn't so hard. But it was hard. Julie knew that. Going for your dreams was hard. Suddenly she was struck with an emotion so strong and unpleasant it took her by surprise.

She was jealous.

Jealous of the peace Tony had found. Peace she had been searching for since she was fourteen.

He still felt guilty, but he was moving forward, toward a sense of belonging in a place. She studied the ground at her feet.

She must have made some little sound because Tony stopped midsentence and tightened his grip on her hand. "What's the matter?"

She struggled to clear all the emotion off her face before she looked up at him. "Nothing. Why?"

He opened his mouth, then apparently decided against what he had been about to say, and shrugged. He went back to his description of the barn.

Julie's mind raced. As a teenager she'd hated her time in Ferndale so much. She'd been so sure she would find her place in a big city. But she hadn't really found herself there, she had just succeeded in losing herself.

Julie suspected there was a big difference.

Chapter Ten

Tony came into the kitchen as Julie, half awake, was muttering to herself and wiping down the counter after she'd slopped coffee.

"I have to go to Santa Rosa for supplies. Want to come?"

"Do I? You bet!" Julie needed to get out of Ferndale. Santa Rosa wasn't exactly a metropolis, but it was a whole lot bigger than Ferndale.

Tony looked surprised at her enthusiasm. "You been too long without a trip to the lumberyard?" He grinned at her.

Julie tossed a sponge at him. "If I go we have to make a few other stops."

Tony immediately looked suspicious. "What kind of stops and how many?"

"What? You don't want to stand outside the dressing room and hold my purse while I try on clothes?"

Julie laughed at the pained looked on his face. "I'm kidding. But I do want to stop at a supermarket. And I need some toiletries from a big drugstore. Can you handle that?"

Tony looked relieved. "Yeah. I can handle that."

"And lunch. I'm dying for Chinese."

Tony nodded. "Lunch. Sure."

"When do you want to leave?"

"As soon as you can be ready. I'm stalled here on the bath upstairs and at my place, too. So today is a loss for work until I can get the supplies I need. And it's a three-hour drive each way."

"Help yourself to coffee. I'll be down in five minutes." Julie raced up the stairs, changed out of her work shirt and shorts and threw on a flowered sundress.

The weather report this morning had promised a hot day and the only air-conditioning in Tony's truck came in through the open windows. Besides, the dress was the most flattering thing she had brought to Ferndale and she hadn't had a chance to wear something without paint on it for weeks.

She pulled a brush through her hair. Even though her collarbone was mending well she still couldn't manage a decent ponytail, so she left her hair down.

True to her word, she was back downstairs in record time. When Tony turned from the kitchen window and she saw the look of admiration on his face, she was glad she had chosen the dress.

"I'm ready. I just need to grab a bottle of water." Julie opened the door of the fridge and leaned in. "You want one?"

She thought she heard Tony groan. When she glanced over her shoulder he was dragging both his hands down his face. She straightened up, concerned. "You okay?"

He gave her a pained smile. "Yeah. I'm great."

What the heck was wrong with him? she wondered. "Do you want water?" She held up a bottle.

Yeah, Tony though as he nodded. Just dump it over my

head. When she'd bent over in that short little dress, he thought he might swallow his tongue.

He grabbed the bottles out of her hand and headed out the door. "Let's go."

Julie grabbed her purse and followed Tony out to his truck. Manners dictated that he help her in, but for his own sanity he kept his eyes fastened on the top of her head and not on the expanse of leg that she bared as she made the big step up into the passenger seat. He closed the door and heaved a sigh of relief.

The traffic wasn't too bad and they made good time going south, chatting about the projects still remaining.

When they reached the outskirts of Santa Rosa, Julie said, "When do you think it will be safe to list the house? I don't want potential buyers to have to step over tarps and around sawhorses."

His gut tightened and his hands gripped the steering wheel. The fierce reaction to her question took Tony by surprise. He didn't want to talk about her selling the house because that would mean she would return to L.A.

He wouldn't see her again.

He had been racking his brain to come up with a way to convince Julie to stay in Ferndale, but nothing had come to mind.

"Tony? Did you hear me?"

He took a deep breath. "Yeah. I was just thinking. It will still take a couple of weeks to do the window frames and the yard. You still want to do the yard, don't you?"

"I'd like to clean it up, but nothing fancy."

"If we get some grass seed and a sprinkler, we can pull the dead shrubs out and at least green up the lawn. That should help a lot." He felt foolish coming up with ideas to make the house sell, when he needed her to have that last tie to Ferndale.

She nodded. "And get rid of the wash line."

He turned his head to glance at her. "I could use that at my place. I'll trade you the labor for the poles."

She laughed. "You going to use it to dry laundry or for chin-ups?"

"You been watching me?" The thought of her watching him warmed him right up.

Julie blushed. "I, ah, yes."

The silence became charged with energy. Had he not been driving, he would have grabbed her and kissed her silly. Instead he had to settle for glances in between watching the road.

He couldn't resist teasing her. "You're blushing."

Her hand fluttered up toward her face and then back into her lap. "No, I'm not!"

He gave her a smug smile. "Sure you are. You liked what you saw."

"I...I...."

Tony grinned at her. Her cheeks had turned a becoming shade of pink. "I left you speechless."

She glared at him. "You have a giant ego."

"Nope, just good powers of observation."

The conversation dropped as he turned into the parking lot of the lumberyard. He pulled into a spot next to the door. "You want to stay in the truck?"

All of a sudden he wasn't sure he wanted her in a lumberyard office in her sexy little dress.

She looked wistfully at the building. "Is it air-conditioned in there?"

He shrugged. "I think so."

She scooted over to get to her door. "I'll go in with you."

Her skirt rode up her thighs. He had to swallow hard and look away before he said, "Suit yourself."

He came around to open the door for her, but she was

already sliding out of the truck, her skirt riding up higher than should be allowable by law.

Tony positioned himself between Julie and the bank of windows across the front of the office, then made a grab for her good arm as she made contact with the asphalt.

He had no intention of letting go of her. "This shouldn't take long. I called the order in while you were getting changed."

Julie smiled up at him and he melted. "No problem."

He held the door for her and heard her sigh as they were hit with a blast of cool air. He didn't want her to be uncomfortable in a hot truck, but he didn't much like the appreciative glances of the men waiting by the service desk.

He knew what they were thinking, because it was the same thing he had been thinking when she had walked into her kitchen in her dress.

As they waited by the service desk for his turn, Julie pulled away from him and wandered over to a rack of how-to books. Short of looking like a caveman and hauling her back to his side, there was nothing he could do. He settled for glaring at every guy who stared at her.

Tony paid for his order and caught up with Julie. She was looking at a book on building decks.

He touched her arm. She looked up at him, then smiled and held up the book. "I can't seem to help myself."

"You thinking about building a deck?"

"No, but it would look great on the back of your place."

Tony was thrilled that she had been thinking about his place. He pictured her there daily, and wanted her to do the same. It was a step in the right direction.

He answered her as she returned the book to the rack. "Eventually. I have all kinds of plans."

She nodded and put the book back on the rack.

"We have to drive around to the back and pick up the lumber."

They left the cool office and climbed back into the hot truck. Tony drove to the will call area of the lot and helped the men load up the order, then he pulled out of the lot.

He heard her stomach rumble. "Hungry?"

She put her hand over her belly and laughed. "Starving!"

"One of the guys in the yard said there was a great Chinese place over by the Yard Bird store."

"Great. Let's go."

They found the restaurant and when they entered the dark interior, Julie inhaled the wonderful scents. "Ah, this smells great."

They slid into a booth and Tony noticed that almost all the other customers were Chinese. A good sign, he thought.

Their waiter arrived with menus and a pot of tea. The menus were filled with much more traditional Chinese dishes than most restaurants.

Julie pointed to the menu. "I don't know what half this stuff is."

"What are you hungry for?"

"I love almond chicken, or orange chicken. Or anything with mushrooms."

"Let me order for us." He was familiar with some of the dishes after spending time in southeast Asia.

She looked skeptical. "What are you going to order?"

He pointed out several dishes and told her what they were.

"How do you know that?"

"I spent time in Hong Kong when I was in the Navy."

"That must have been interesting for a guy who hates cities."

"Julie, I don't hate cities. I just don't want to live in one."

She shrugged one bare smooth shoulder. "Were you on vacation?"

"I had some leave coming and the team was in Indonesia. A couple of us decided to visit Hong Kong before we came home."

"I've always wanted to travel, but China won't be in the budget for a long time." She sounded wistful.

The longing note in her voice made him want to take what was left in his bank account and buy tickets for the next flight.

Man, he had it bad. And it frightened him, because he had no idea how she felt about him.

The waiter came and took their order. While they waited for their food Tony told her about seeing Hong Kong. He and Jimmy had taken in the sights for almost a week before they caught a flight back to the States.

She told him about all the places she wanted to visit.

After they finished lunch they went to two more building supply stores and then the drugstore.

Julie looked up as they came out of the drug store and spotted a bookstore across the street.

"How are we doing for time?"

Tony tossed the bag in the back of the truck. "Why?"

"I'd like to make a quick trip in the bookstore."

"We have time." He took her arm and waited for traffic to clear.

Julie made a beeline for the children's section and ran her eyes quickly over the titles. She always checked the inventory, looking for books similar to the ones she planned to write. She pulled a few off the shelf and checked the publishers, mentally filing away the information. When she was ready to send her manuscript, she would know who to target.

A display of Harry Potter books caught her eye. She turned and studied Tony.

He glanced up and saw her looking at him. "What?"

Would a big macho guy like him be willing to read a

children's book? "Have you heard of Harry Potter?" She picked up the first book in the series.

He gave her a look that said she'd asked a really silly question. "Julie, everybody's heard of Harry Potter. I live in Ferndale, not on the moon."

She laughed. "I haven't read them yet, but I need to. The author targets the same age group I'm after." She hesitated. Would he be insulted? "Would you like to read it to me?"

"Sure we can't start with Clancy or King?" He sounded hopeful.

She shuddered. "I don't read horror. Clancy might be okay." Actually the plot might be too complicated to read just a little at a time, but she wanted him to be comfortable with the material.

He laughed. "Harry Potter's fine. I've been curious about the books, with all the press it's been getting."

Julie carried the book to the checkout stand and paid for it. It was rare that she left a bookstore with only one book, but between the state of her finances and the long drive home, they needed to get going.

They made a final stop at the supermarket, then headed back to Ferndale.

She'd had fun, Julie thought as Tony pulled onto the highway. They hadn't done anything special and nothing exciting had happened, but the day had been wonderful. She enjoyed being with Tony. Anyone watching them would have thought they were a couple.

She realized how much she was going to miss him when she went back to L.A.

She let her mind wander. What if he came to L.A. and found he liked it? She wondered if he would give the city a fair chance. She began to daydream about the things she would show him and the places they could go.

As they pulled off the highway on the road towards Ferndale, she was glad to see the lights of the town twinkling in the distance. It had been a long day, and it felt good to come back.

The thought startled her and she sat up straight and stared out the windshield.

She must be more tired than she thought.

"All work and no play makes Julie a dull girl."

Amused, Julie, paint roller in hand, turned to Tony. "Well, thanks. I was shooting for boring, but I guess I'll settle for dull."

He pulled the paint roller out of her hand and slipped it into a Ziploc bag. It was getting to be a regular occurrence. At first his in-charge attitude had annoyed her, but she enjoyed their outings too much to fight him.

He caught her hand and tugged her toward the stairs. "Come on, it's an incredible day and we need to get out of here. Besides, you can't put a second coat on that wall until the first one dries."

She pretended to pout as she followed after him. It had become part of the game. "You're worse than some of my hyperactive students."

But better looking. Oh so much better looking!

"Yeah, well, I've heard worse." He paused at her bedroom door. "Change into shorts and a T-shirt, and bring a sweatshirt. I'll meet you downstairs."

As a fashion consultant he had a long way to go. She knew she should be working, but she'd been feeling a little down. The closer they got to finishing the house, the bluer she felt. It was always like this for her. A letdown. Maybe Tony was right. It was a beautiful day and a break was what she needed.

Julie changed and hurried downstairs. Tony was throwing food and water bottles in a ratty backpack.

"How many days are we going to be gone?" She asked, eyeing the food.

"Such a comedian. Don't worry. I'll carry the backpack."

"You bet you will. And if things get too tough, you'll be carrying me."

"Come on, don't turn into a wimpy city girl on me."

"Hey, cowboy, don't look now, but I *am* a wimpy city girl."

His eyes traveled down her body. The look he gave her made her blood sing.

She cleared her throat. "Are we ready?"

"Oh, yeah," he said, waggling his eyebrows.

She laughed. "You are hopeless."

"Not entirely, but I'm working on it." He frowned down at her sneakers. "Are those the best shoes you have?"

"No, the best shoes I have are a pair of Ferragamo pumps, but I thought these would be better for hiking," she said sweetly.

He was wearing boots. She didn't own boots. At least not the hiking kind.

"Where are we going?"

"Fern Canyon."

They took her car. As they drove in on the dirt road, their wheels sent up great clouds of dust. All the ferns along the access road were gray with fine silt, giving the approach to the canyon a strange, otherworldly look.

They emerged at the coast, between high cliffs and the ocean. Julie spotted some huge Roosevelt Elk grazing on the beach grass.

"Tony, look." She grabbed his arm and pointed.

He nodded. "This is whole area is a reserve."

She continued to stare at the magnificent animals as Tony parked in the tiny lot at the base of Fern Canyon, across from one other car. Again Julie was struck by how deserted it was.

Tony hitched on the backpack and headed for the trail that started at the edge of the parking lot. The canyon floor was fairly level, but the steep sides looked to be as high as a hundred feet, thick with lush green ferns.

He set a pace up the trail that had the muscles in her calves burning within a half hour. She really needed to get home and back to her regular workouts at the gym.

He wasn't even winded.

The canyon was beautiful. Covered with many varieties of ferns and tall redwoods, very little sunlight filtered down to the canyon floor. It gave Julie a feeling almost like being underwater. It reminded her of some of the forest scenes from one of the *Star Wars* movies.

There were charming little wooden bridges over trickling streams, and here and there they had to skirt boulders and fallen trees. Small rivulets of water ran off the canyon walls like miniature waterfalls.

Aside from the tiny black gnats that seemed determined to fly up her nose, it was an idyllic place. There wasn't another person around. It was as if the forest belonged to them alone.

After another twenty minutes of steady walking, Julie needed a break. She grabbed a hold of the end of a piece of strapping hanging off Tony's backpack and gave it a tug. Before she could blink, he swung around in a crouch, his hands up in a defensive position, his eyes cold and flat.

Startled by the suddenness of his reaction, she stumbled back a step.

Tony stood up and extended a hand to her, a look of distress on his face. "Sorry. Didn't mean to scare you."

"I wasn't scared." And with a bolt of realization, she realized she never would be frightened when she was with Tony. He was the most capable man she had ever known.

She couldn't imagine a situation he couldn't handle. But she also knew he would never hurt her.

She smiled to reassure him. "I wanted a drink of water."

He studied her for a moment. "You need to rest? You look a little flushed."

Her pride wouldn't let her admit she was getting tired. "No, I'm just thirsty."

He shrugged the pack off his shoulders and unzipped the main compartment. He handed her a bottle of water and took one for himself. After he popped open the spout he tipped his head back and took a long drink. Julie watched the muscles in his neck as he swallowed. Then he squirted water over his face, dragging up the hem of his shirt to mop up his face. His toned belly with its ridges of muscle made her want to reach out and touch.

Oh, brother. She went warm all over and wondered if she might be experiencing her first hot flash.

Down girl, she thought.

He was off-limits and she intended to stick to that plan. It was working great and she didn't want to mess it up.

Julie smacked the spout closed on her bottle and stuck it back in the pack. Best to keep moving.

"I'm ready." She handed the bottle back to Tony.

He stuffed both water bottles back in the pack. "You sure? We're not in any hurry, are we?"

Julie shrugged out of her sweatshirt and tied it around her waist. "I do want to finish the dining-room walls today."

"Okay." He took off up the path.

Julie tried really hard not to watch his fine-looking rear end as she followed him.

Tony turned off the main path onto a smaller trail. "I want you to see the view. We'll eat when we get to the top. Then we can head back."

"Okay." Julie followed him as the path began to climb.

So far they had been walking on a relatively flat trail, but now they were gaining altitude steadily, and he didn't slow the pace.

Even though he teased her about being a city girl, she had her pride. She struggled to keep up with his long-legged stride until her lungs burned and her legs ached.

Finally she had to give in. "Tony," she gasped. "Wait."

He turned and gave her an amused look. "We're almost there."

"I'm wiped out. Give me a minute." She fixed him with a look. "And don't laugh at me."

He held out both hands, wiping all expression off his face. "I'm not laughing."

Julie bent over and braced both her hands on her knees, taking in deep breaths. She peered up at him. "But you want to."

"Come on, you put on the backpack." He shrugged the straps off his shoulders.

She straightened up and shot him an incredulous look. "I'm dying here and you want me to carry that ton of food you packed?"

He stepped around behind her and slid the backpack up onto her shoulders. "You carry this and I'll carry you."

She turned to face him. "I was kidding about that!"

"So? You think I can't?"

She wondered if he realized he looked like a little kid who had been offered a dare when he stuck his chin out like that.

"I'm too heavy." And the hill they were climbing was plenty steep.

"I carried packs up to a hundred and twenty pounds in the service. And I'm in as good shape now as I was then." There was a belligerent edge to his tone inviting her to challenge him.

No way was she going to step on his ego by challenging

his strength. If he wanted to prove something to her she could play along.

"Okay." She said sweetly. "What do you plan to do? Heave me over your shoulder?" She gave him her best "I'm just the little woman" look.

His expression serious, he shook his head. He didn't realize she was teasing him.

"No." He turned his back. "Hop on. I'll take you piggyback."

She had an instantaneous flash to her childhood. Her dad used to carry her piggyback when she'd get tired. As silly as it was, she wanted to do that again.

"Okay." She put her hands on his shoulders and jumped onto his back.

He caught the backs of her thighs and hoisted her up until her legs were around his middle. She grabbed hold of his shoulders as he clasped his hands together under her bottom and headed up the trail.

As soon as Tony started to walk Julie realized she had made a grave tactical error.

She went into sensual overload.

With her legs stretched wide around his waist and his hands pushed up under her bottom, every step he took brought her into a close contact of the tantalizing kind.

She wrapped her arms around his neck and hung on for dear life, only to have her breasts rub against his back. She had to remind herself to breathe occasionally. When she did, the air she drew in smelled of him.

He kept up a steady pace and she prayed they didn't have far to go because she wasn't sure how much of this heightened awareness she was going to be able to tolerate.

She felt like she was on fire.

As the foliage began to thin, Julie noticed Tony's breathing had increased with his exertion, and the back of his neck was slick with perspiration. She had the urge to lick his skin.

Julie swallowed and counted to ten, trying to think up lesson plans to keep her mind off him.

It didn't work.

She had to get down, now, or do something really stupid and make a fool of herself.

"Ah, Tony."

"Yeah," he grunted.

"I can walk now."

"You sure?" He shifted his hands.

A bolt of pure sensation shot up through her body.

"I'm sure," she managed to say on a strangled exhale.

He paused by a huge redwood stump and backed up until she was sitting, then let go of her. She let her arms drop from his shoulders and took a deep breath, trying to compose herself.

Instead of stepping forward, away from her, he turned, still in the lee of her legs, and slid an arm around her waist, yanking her up against the front of his jeans.

She'd assumed she was the only one affected.

She'd been wrong.

Before she could say anything he shoved his other hand into her hair and tugged her up for a kiss she felt all the way to her toes.

Sensation swirled through her and she kissed him back. She circled her arms around his chest and opened her mouth under his insistent lips, angling her head so that he could deepen the kiss.

She felt his hand leave her head and pull at the sweatshirt tied around her waist. He loosened it enough so he could run his hand up under her shirt.

The feel of his work-roughened palm on the bare skin of her back ratcheted her pulse up another level.

As he stroked closer and closer to her breast, she almost cried in frustration, she wanted him there so much.

She ripped his shirt from the waistband of his jeans so she could get her hands on all the lovely muscles of his back she had been watching for the last month.

Just as his hand closed over her breast, he stiffened and went still. The sound of voices drifted down from the ridge right above them.

He drew his hand away from her skin and broke the kiss, muttering a frustrated obscenity into her hair.

Tony stepped back but the air around them still seemed charged by their need and attraction. He quickly bent and retied her sweatshirt around her waist while she ran her fingers through her hair.

Within seconds a man and two teenage boys came into sight. They exchanged greetings and the threesome walked on by.

Tony sank down onto the opposite side of the stump. She turned so she could see him.

Without looking at her he said, "Julie, I'm sorry."

"Sorry?" His words stung. It had been wonderful. Why was he sorry?

"Yeah. I lost control."

"Ah. A mortal sin," she said waspishly, physical need still clawing at her.

He glanced over at her. "I thought we had a kind of unspoken agreement." His voice was quiet and pensive.

She sighed. He was right, of course. Getting involved physically would change everything, and not for the better.

"That's true," she agreed reluctantly.

"And besides that, this was not the place." He gestured to the path. "If we'd gone any further...." his voice trailed off.

We might have found heaven, Julie thought as she nodded in agreement. No one had ever made her feel like Tony just had.

She had the sneaking suspicion that she was half in love with him, and that was the best reason of all for not letting what had just occurred to happen again.

Because she had no intention of falling in love with anyone.

Ever.

Chapter Eleven

Julie hung up the phone after trying unsuccessfully to placate the furious manager of her apartment building. The nineteen-year-olds subletting her place had thrown a party that had gotten out of hand and the manager had been forced to call the police. Now he was demanding that Julie come back and evict her tenants and repair any damage, or he would break her lease.

She rubbed at her temple where a throbbing had begun. She should've known better to leave her apartment to a couple of teenagers, even if she worked with their sister.

She wondered if her collarbone was healed enough to make the drive. Julie stood up and flexed her arm. Only one way to find out.

Grabbing her keys off the hook by the kitchen door, she went out back. She pulled the cover off her car and stuffed it into the trunk.

She slid into the driver's seat, and realized she couldn't touch the pedals. Tony had been the last one to drive. To Fern Canyon.

Julie laid her head against the steering wheel and let the memories of their hike up the canyon two days ago flash through her mind, igniting her body all over again.

She straightened up, steeling herself against the recollections. Best not to dwell on what she wouldn't allow herself.

She adjusted the seat, started the car and drove down to the end of Main Street, around back past the school and home. She shifted gears about a dozen times and her shoulder was aching by the time she pulled up in front of the house.

She sat in the driver's seat wondering how much a ticket from the Arcata airport to L.A. was going to cost her. Probably about as much as shrubs and grass for the yard, she thought glumly.

Tony pulled up behind her and parked his truck. She hadn't seen him for two days and had to admit she'd missed him. He looked mighty good.

He unfolded his tall frame and stood waiting for her. "Out for a joyride?"

She opened the door and climbed out. "Not much joy." She winced as she flexed her arm.

"Still pretty sore?" The concern creasing his brow touched her.

"Yeah. Shifting gears is tough. And I have to go to L.A. tomorrow."

He raised an eyebrow. "How come?"

Julie explained the telephone call from her landlord.

He shook his head in sympathy. "Want me to drive you down?"

"I can't ask you to do that." His offer surprised her. She knew how he felt about spending time in the city.

He gave her a steady look. "You didn't. I offered."

"Are you sure?" Had she ever met such a nice guy? She didn't think so.

"Sure. Betty will be home this weekend, so I don't have to worry about her place."

She felt a little tingle of excitement. This would be her chance to show him there were some good points to living in a city. "So, cowboy, you're ready for a visit to the big city?"

"Sure. You make it sound like I've never been out of a small town. Don't forget I lived in Annapolis while I went to the Academy and then I took my SEAL training in San Diego."

"But you've never *lived* there. Being in training or on a college campus is different. I'm talking about a grown-up, out-on-your-own living."

He laughed. "No. If you're going to put those kinds of conditions on it, I haven't."

"If you come with me this weekend, I'll show you the good side of living in a city."

He gave her a serious look. "For you, I'll try to like it."

For some reason his comment made her uneasy, but she smiled at him. She was just being silly. He'd probably hate L.A.

Julie glanced over at Tony. The trip to L.A. was not off to a good start.

A snarl of traffic on Highway 99 South due to a five-car accident had them sitting in traffic for three hours, and they were still in the Central Valley, not even to Fresno yet.

Julie had chosen the inland route because it was quicker.

Tony didn't seemed bothered by the traffic jam, but his fingers drummed on the steering wheel. She knew him well enough to know the enforced boredom was not something he tolerated well. She admired him for not mentioning the delay.

He seemed to feel her staring at him and turned his head

and smiled. ''What are you going to do with your renters when we get there?''

She raised one brow. ''You mean after I throw them out?'' She was still furious at herself for renting to them.

He shifted the car into first gear and rolled forward about twenty feet. ''No second chances?''

Julie shook her head. ''According to the manager they were way beyond second chances. He's already warned them twice.''

He shifted in his seat. ''Do you think they'll cause trouble?''

''No. I sublet to Robert, but his sister and I work together. I figure he'll leave quietly, especially if I don't make a big deal out of this to Elaine.''

He laughed. ''Big sisters can have that kind of effect on a guy.''

''Especially Elaine. Did your older sister try to keep you in line?'' She turned in her seat as much as the seat belt would allow.

Tony grinned. ''It was her sole occupation as a teenager.''

He had such a wonderful smile. ''Was she successful?''

He sent her an amused look. ''What do you think?''

Julie fiddled with the radio, trying to get rid of the static. ''I think you probably went out of your way to annoy her.''

''Yup. It was my job. Little brothers are duty bound to annoy older sisters.''

Julie wished she'd had a younger brother. Then there would have been someone to share what had happened when her folks died. Someone who would understand what she'd been through. Someone to suffer through squares of lime Jell-O with shredded carrots and canned chicken noodle soup every Sunday after church.

Tony put his free hand on her shoulder. ''Hey, where did you go?''

She smiled over at him. "Just remembering what it was like to be a teenager."

"Good memories, or bad?"

"Are teenage memories ever good?" she asked with a laugh.

He studied her for a moment. "Yeah. Sometimes they are, if you're lucky."

Julie sensed Tony was one of the lucky ones. She decided to change the subject. "So what do you want to do when we get to L.A.?"

He gazed out at the endless line of traffic ahead of them. "Are we ever going to get to L.A.?"

"Sure. This is just one of those *unavoidable* things, right?"

"You're the tour director. Your job is to show me the good side of the city."

"Right." Tony would enjoy the outdoorsy things to do. They would definitely have to spend time at the beach.

His voice cut into her thoughts. "Do you ever surf?"

"No. Always wanted to try it, though." She had a secret weakness for teenage beach blanket movies. Everyone ended up happy.

"How about windsurf? Have you ever been windsurfing?"

She nodded. "Did a little in Hawaii." Not well, but at least she had tried it.

"We could do that."

She ignored the little voice that was telling her the water at Redondo would be a whole lot colder than it was in Hawaii.

"There's a place not too far from my apartment that rents gear. We could spend the day tomorrow at the beach, then go to dinner and a movie, maybe into Hollywood. I miss the movies."

Tony nodded in agreement. "That sounds like fun."

"And I want you to see the mountains. There are some great trails up in the Angeles Crest. We could hike on Sunday."

"Are these the things you'd be doing if I wasn't with you?"

Julie hesitated. She'd never been hiking in the mountains. But it sounded like a good idea. "Well, to tell the truth I'd probably go shopping. But that didn't sound like your kind of activity."

"If you want to shop, we can." He adopted the air of a martyr.

Julie laughed. "Let's save that in case it rains. And you're pretty safe. It hasn't rained in L.A. in the summer for years."

Finally the traffic began to move and Tony kept his attention on the road. By the time they got to the site of the accident all they saw were the remains of burned out flares and probably a ton of squashed tomatoes littering the side of the road. Julie was relieved there was nothing to see. Ever since her parents' death she had not been able to understand the rubber-necking people did at accident sites. It was too personal to her.

That was so typical of a huge traffic snarl like this one. It took so much time to clear the backup of cars that the evidence was pretty much gone when you got there. The only clue here was the ripe fruit left behind.

Since they were driving back on Monday they shouldn't hit as much traffic. "On the way back we can take the coastal route. It's not as fast, but a lot more scenic."

They stopped to stretch their legs in Fresno, then pushed through to L.A.

Julie had booked two rooms at the budget motel near her apartment, but they decided to go to her place first even though it was after eleven. From what her apartment manager had said, the young men who sublet her place were just getting revved up by then.

They found a parking place out front and walked in past the pool. Julie knocked on the door, glad Tony was with her.

There was no answer. She used her key to open the door and flipped on the light. The place was deserted and smelled like a brewery. They moved through the apartment. It was obvious the guys had moved out.

"Did they know you were coming?" Tony asked as he headed back to the living room.

"I didn't call them, but I suppose the manager let them know."

"Yeah," Tony said, bending over to examine a large stain on the living-room floor, "Chickens. They decided not to stand and fight."

Julie walked over beside him. "Ugh. What do you suppose that is. Or was?"

"Keg of beer. See the indented ring on the carpet? That's where the tub was. It's still damp. They must have thrown themselves a going-away party."

She opened the two windows in the living room to get some air in the place. "Remind me to go apologize to the neighbors."

"Do you think this will hurt your relationships with people in the building?" Tony was examining a fresh patch in the plaster wall by the kitchen.

Julie shook her head. She didn't know the people in her building, except to say hello at the mailboxes. "I don't think it will be a problem."

The place was dirty and smelly, but Julie was thankful the damage looked to be minimal.

Tony took her by the arm. "I'll cancel your room at the motel. You can stay here."

There he was again, taking charge. Wasn't this trip supposed to be her doing? She pulled out of his grasp because she liked it too much.

"I'm going to cancel both rooms. If you don't mind staying here with me." Just to make things clear she pointed to the sofa and said, "The Hide-A-Bed is pretty comfortable."

"That would be fine. We can get the place cleaned up in no time."

"Oh, no. We are *not* going to spend this weekend cleaning the apartment. We're here to see the city and have fun. Are you hungry?"

Tony glanced at the clock in the kitchen. "Yeah, but it's after eleven."

"Not a problem. They might roll up the sidewalks in Ferndale at night, but there are plenty of places to eat here at midnight."

They carried their bags in and then they went back to the car. She directed him to a little restaurant down by the water that specialized in seafood and pasta.

The pasta Tony had made the week before was better, but dinner was okay.

When they got back to the apartment, Julie was exhausted.

Tony glanced out at the pool. "Okay with you if I go for a swim?"

"Aren't you tired?" After all, he had driven the whole way.

"Yeah, but I need to get some of the kinks out before I try to sleep."

"Sure, go ahead. I'm tired." She handed him the keys. "I'll get you a pillow and a blanket."

By the time Julie returned to the living room Tony was gone. She made up the couch and then wandered over to the living-room window. She could see Tony in the pool, his long arms and strong legs propelling him through the still water. He swam like he was born in the water, his fluid motions pushing him to the end of the pool, graceful turns against the side never breaking his stride.

He was so beautiful. She finally understood the old phrase, poetry in motion. For a minute she let herself remember the way his body had felt against hers when they had hiked Fern Canyon. Dangerous feelings rose up and she ruthlessly tamped them down.

She wanted to show him L.A., so he wouldn't have such a negative view of the city life. She wanted to broaden his horizons. But she didn't expect it to change the path either of them were taking.

And their paths were separate.

She tore her eyes away from Tony and wrote a note to the apartment manager and slipped it under his door, then came back and crawled into bed.

She lay awake. Tony came in and used the shower. Everything got quiet. She lay awake for a long time.

The next morning they stopped for coffee and muffins at the coffee shop on the corner and then rented a windsurfing board. They left their towels on the beach. It became apparent as soon as they got in the water that she hadn't mastered the sport in Hawaii, and with her sore collarbone she wasn't going to today, either.

Tony spent the morning in the water. Julie watched him from the sand. He made it look so easy.

By ten o'clock the water was so crowded he could hardly find room to maneuver. By eleven the water had become so congested with Jet Skis and kayaks and other windsurfers he had to give up and come in.

Good thing, Julie thought. "I'm starving. How about lunch?"

They returned the rented board and picked up their towels. When they got back to the car, Julie noticed glass on the rear deck behind the back seat.

Someone had broken into her car.

"There was nothing to take!" She wailed, furious at the invasion.

Tony motioned to the car next to them. "You weren't the only one. Look."

"The beach is full of people. How could they do this in broad daylight and not have anyone notice?"

He rubbed her back in a sympathetic gesture. "Maybe people did notice and figured it wasn't their problem."

The thought was depressing. He was probably right.

Gently he took her arm. "There's a pay phone. Do you want me to call the police?"

Julie knew they wouldn't respond to a car break-in. "No, there's nothing they can do."

"There's a glass place on the way to your apartment. Let's stop and see how long it will take to fix it."

He noticed that? *She'd* never noticed that. Dispirited she said, "Okay."

They pulled in and were told they would have to leave the car for two hours. Julie gave her insurance information to the manager. He asked where the car had been parked and told them break-ins happened every summer.

As they walked home Tony said, "The glass place seems to have the perfect location."

"I suppose." Julie hated the thought of the money she would have to shell out for the deductible on her insurance. Plus, with her renters gone, she'd have to pay next month's rent, too.

"Hey, you're not going to let this spoil the day, are you?"

She looked up at him, realizing their roles had changed. She had envisioned herself as the cheerleader this weekend. She managed to dredge up a smile for him. "No."

Julie showered first, then changed into clean clothes. She cleaned part of the kitchen while Tony took his turn in the bathroom. She wasn't going to ruin his weekend by letting him help her clean.

They went to a wood fire pizza place for lunch. By the time they were finished Julie felt much better. As they walked back to pick up the car she realized how hot and smoggy the day had become. The heat from the pavement radiated up through her sandals.

She wasn't sure she was up to any more physical activities. "How about we go to the movies? There's a multiplex at the mall."

"Is this a sneaky plot to go shopping?" He gave her a suspicious look.

Julie laughed. "No. I promise." And held up fingers in the Girl Scout salute.

She directed Tony to the mall. While they circled for almost fifteen minutes looking a parking place in the underground parking structure they discussed which movie they wanted to see. They agreed on an action film. It wasn't Julie's first choice, but the weekend was not going as well as she hoped, so she silently decided she owed Tony.

The movie they'd agreed on was sold out. Her first choice didn't start for another hour, so they settled for one neither of them knew anything about that started in five minutes.

By the time they got into the theater, the lights were off and most of the seats were filled. They made their way down front and settled in.

The movie was a hopeless teenage comedy the audience found enthralling because they were as moronic as the actors on the screen. Julie endured almost two hours of rude noises and jokes about body functions. Most of the noises came from the kids sitting around them.

Yuck, she thought watching the idiotic plot wind to a close. She wondered how Tony was taking it.

She didn't have the nerve to lean over and ask him.

For her it was like being in the classroom. She wouldn't have been surprised when the lights came on to see the audience filled with her students.

As the credits filled the screen, Tony tapped her on the arm. She turned and he slid his hand around her nape and gave her a toe-curling kiss, all lips and tongue and vibrating sensation.

"What did you do that for?" she asked in a breathy whisper when he finally let her go.

The lights came on and he hauled her up out of her chair, heading for the exit. "Just didn't want the last two hours to be a complete loss."

She couldn't think of anything to say as they walked out.

The mall was teeming with the usual Saturday-evening crowd. Tony looked uncomfortable as he shifted from foot to foot. "What do you want to do now?"

She wanted to tease him about shopping, but he looked so antsy she decided not to push it.

"How about we take a walk along the beach? My favorite restaurant is about a half mile from my apartment."

Tony looked relieved at the suggestion. "Sure thing."

They made their way back to the car and headed back toward the beach. They parked at her apartment and walked down to the beach, then along the sand until they got to the restaurant. Trash left behind during the day littered the beach.

Julie couldn't help but think of the pristine empty beaches near Ferndale. Tony was polite enough not to voice a comparison, but she knew he couldn't help but notice.

Dinner was a two-hour wait. She should have realized. It was Saturday night. No one in L.A. seemed to stay home on Saturday night.

After dinner they returned to Julie's apartment. "Tomorrow we can drive up into the mountains and take a hike."

"I'd like that. Want to talk for a while?" Tony gestured to the couch.

After that kiss in the theater and two glasses of wine with dinner she didn't think that was a good idea. "Actually I'm pretty tired. I think I'll turn in." She wasn't sure she would be able to resist temptation.

It took her a long time to fall asleep knowing he was in the next room. On her couch. Probably close to naked.

Julie groaned and rolled over. Why had she decided to broaden Tony's horizons? It had become torture for her.

The next morning they drove up the Angeles Crest highway and pulled off into a full parking lot. The trails were jammed with people. Julie spent the entire time they walked thinking of the beauty and solitude of Fern Canyon.

What a joke, she thought as she packed to make the trip back up the coast early Monday morning. She had tried to show Tony how wonderful a city could be, and had failed miserably.

Now she didn't like small towns and she wasn't sure she liked cities, either.

She felt like she had when she'd been fourteen. She didn't really belong anywhere.

When they pulled away from her apartment building she turned to look at him. He had been such a good sport all weekend. "Tony, I'm sorry."

He looked surprised. "For what?"

She shook her head in amazement. "For the weekend. It was awful."

He glanced at her. "Would you be offended if I told you it was just about what I expected?"

She considered his statement for a moment. "No. But I wanted you to enjoy it."

"I did."

She laughed. "Which part? The smog, or the crowds? Or maybe waiting half the night to eat?"

''I enjoyed it because I spent it with you.''

Her heart skipped a beat when it shouldn't have. She didn't know what to say, so she simply said, ''Thank you.''

As they drove up the spectacular coastal route, Julie realized the best part of the trip to L.A. was going back.

Chapter Twelve

Julie filled another cardboard box with old books and ledgers from her grandfather's business. She hadn't seen Tony since he had lifted all the junk down out of the top of the closets for her. He had been out at his place for the last two days working on his house.

She missed him. She didn't want or need the feelings. She'd be leaving soon and heading home for good.

For good. Interesting phrase.

She tried to shake her gloomy mood. The trip to show Tony Los Angeles had been a disaster. He'd been very polite over the weekend, but she knew he'd had a miserable time, in spite of his sweet comment about being with her.

All the things she had wanted to show him had not worked out. She would have loved to say the crowds and the traffic and the smog were a fluke, but she knew better. She had always considered them the price you had to pay for living in the city.

Now she wondered what the reward was.

She opened a carton labeled Julie and found her high

school yearbook on top. Aside from a little dust on the cover it looked new.

She remembered when her homeroom teacher had handed it to her. She hadn't wanted it. She'd already been accepted to college and couldn't wait to get out of Ferndale. She hadn't understood all the tears and nostalgia of the other students.

She set the book aside and under it was a bound book of blank pages. Her mother had given it to her as a Christmas gift just before the accident that had killed her parents. She'd been thrilled with the gift. At the time she wrote poetry and secretly decided this would hold her first volume of poems.

She held the book for a moment and stroked the cover, then opened it to read what her mother had written on the inside cover.

"Write down your thoughts and your feelings, because they are who you are. Love, Mom."

She realized with a start that her parents had been gone now for almost half her life. It hardly seemed possible that it had been that long. She still missed them so much it hurt.

She turned the page to the only poem she had entered in the book. She remembered writing it late on Christmas night when she had been thirteen.

I believe the sun has a spirit of love and honesty.

I believe teardrops dance on the shore of truth and magic.

I believe waves dance and snow breaks against the shore of hopeful wisdom.

I believe windows soar through dark shadows, and bring back a beautiful sailing moon.

I believe snow falls through windows and ash cries in our dark minds.

I believe a window's magic can turn boring skies to

a beautiful world.

I believe that deserted teardrops form a magical island in the path of dreams.

I believe teardrops break our hearts and loving families bring them back together.

Julie closed the book and gave in to her tears. She had
believed in so much back then. Now she knew how much
life could hurt when you lost the people you loved, or you
weren't loved in return.

She was never going to put herself in that position again,
because she was sure she couldn't survive the loss.

She set the book aside and went through the rest of the
carton, not finding anything she was interested in keeping.

The last carton contained a whole set of leather-bound
diaries. She opened the first one and recognized her Grandmother's handwriting. It was dated 1934. Julie did some
quick calculations and realized her grandmother had been
about thirteen when she had started keeping this diary. She
opened all the volumes and then stacked them in order,
from oldest to newest. She read volume after volume, finding out things about Bessie she had never known.

She read Bessie's writing about her own life. How she'd
felt about the way she had been treated by her own parents
and grandparents. Julie began to understand why her grandmother had been so restrictive and reserved. It seemed that
she not only hadn't been allowed to show her feelings, but
she was also chastised for even *having* feelings.

Bessie had been unable to express any love and hated
being touched. Julie had never received as much as a hug
from her grandmother.

Julie stroked the diary with its joyless contents. Maybe
no one had ever hugged Bessie. The thought made her so
sad.

Julie skipped ahead to the diary that her grandmother had

written during the late sixties. After reading about her
grandmother's despair over her mother's teenage years, she
had to smile.

She had never thought of her mother as a teenager, and
apparently her mom had given Bessie a run for her money.

Her mother had once told Julie how much she'd wanted
to get out of Ferndale and go away to school. She had
enrolled at Humbolt State and apparently had never looked
back.

That's where her parents had met. They had run off and
married without their telling their families.

Julie skipped ahead again to the diary her grandmother
kept when Julie's parents died and she'd come to live with
Bessie.

She was surprised at Bessie's grief over her daughter's
death. She'd never shown any sign to Julie that she missed
or grieved for Julie's mom.

Bessie's entries later that year described Julie as rude and
uncommunicative.

She laid the book in her lap.

She supposed she had been. She was hurting so badly
and had been ripped away from the only home she'd ever
known and all her friends and sent to live with a woman
who didn't want her.

Still, it couldn't have been easy for Bessie to take on a
teenager.

Suddenly Julie needed to see Betty. The minister's wife
had known Bessie and could answer some of Julie's questions.

She tucked the diary under her arm and walked the two
blocks to Betty's house. Betty answered the door and immediately drew Julie into a hug. "Oh, honey, it's so good
to see you!"

She pulled Julie into her living room and closed the door.
"How are you?"

"I'm fine, Betty. How was your trip?" The house looked the same as it had fifteen years ago, homey and comfortable.

"Wonderful. But it's always good to come home."

She wondered what that must be like. Julie felt like she hadn't been able to go home for years.

Betty hustled her into the kitchen and made tea, and they settled down at the kitchen table.

Julie put the leather diary on the table with her palm flat on the book. "I was cleaning out closets and came across Bessie's diaries."

"Been taking a trip down memory lane?" Betty asked in a kind voice.

That was an understatement. "Yes. It's been interesting reading."

"How so?" Betty pushed the sugar bowl closer to Julie.

Julie stared into her cup as she stirred her tea. "Oh, the perspective of time, I suppose."

Betty smiled. "Things look a little different than they did when you were fourteen?"

She'd known Betty would understand. "I never considered what it must have been like for Bessie."

Betty shook her head. "She was so scared."

"Scared?" Betty must be mistaken. Bessie had never been scared of anything.

"Oh, yes. Scared she would make the same mistakes with you that she did with your mother."

"What mistakes?" The entries in the diary indicated Bessie thought all the mistakes had been Julie's mom's. And Julie's.

"Did your mother ever talk about her high school years here in Ferndale?"

"Just that she wanted to get out and go away to school. Why?"

"Well, I guess she wouldn't have told you about her last

few years here in Ferndale. It's not the kind of thing a mother tells a young daughter.''

Julie tried to imagine what Betty could be talking about. The mother she remembered was an average suburban housewife. Sensible shoes and a minivan. ''What are you talking about?''

''You have to remember.'' Betty hesitated. ''It was the second half of the sixties, and things were pretty loose and open around here. Drugs were very available and it was the beginning of the sexual revolution.''

Julie was sure Betty must be wrong. Her mom had been president of the PTA. ''Are you sure my mother was involved in that?''

''Oh, honey, the whole high school was. Poor Bessie was overwhelmed, and the wilder your mom got, the stricter Bessie and Herb tried to be. It was a vicious cycle.''

Julie was stunned. ''The whole high school?''

Betty laughed. ''Yes. Some of the most upstanding citizens of Ferndale went to high school with your mom. You'd be amazed at some of the stories I've heard.''

''And Bessie was scared I'd be like my mom?''

''Bessie was scared she didn't know how to raise a child. She didn't have an easy time showing emotion, and you were so devastated when you got here. Not a good combination, I'm afraid.''

Julie nodded in agreement. It hadn't been good. She had thought Bessie didn't love her. It never occurred to her that her grandmother just didn't know how to show that love.

Julie thanked Betty and walked home, seeing Ferndale through different eyes. The whole time she'd lived here all she could think of was leaving. But now she realized it wasn't the town that she didn't like so much as the circumstances that had brought her here. Tony had been right all along.

Tony. She missed him. Would miss him when she left,

more than she wanted to admit. But she would leave, because Tony was a real threat.

She could fall in love with him. And when you loved you could get hurt. The only way to protect yourself was to avoid falling in love in the first place.

Chapter Thirteen

"The house is finished."

Julie stood alone on the sidewalk and said it again, talking to herself.

"The house is finished." The yard was a mess, but that was the easy part.

All summer she thought she'd be delighted to be able to say those words, but they made her feel hollow.

No, just let down, she told herself. After a big project was finished she always felt this way. It had been like this when she had graduated from college. She'd thought she'd feel euphoric, but instead she felt blue.

She shook off the feeling. It was silly, really. After all, she needed to get back home to Los Angeles and get ready for school to start. She still had to teach until the house sold, and who knew how long that would take.

Tony stepped out on the front porch. She ignored the little catch in her heartbeat and gave him a little wave.

He loped down the steps in that loose, easy stride of his and stopped beside her on the sidewalk.

"Admiring your work?"

She plastered a smile on her lips, trying to overcome her melancholy feelings. She didn't like how much she was going to miss him. "Nope. Admiring *your* work. I couldn't have done it without you."

He draped his arm over her shoulder. "Oh, come on. Sure you could. You have all those books," he said with a barely contained smile.

"I'm trying to be serious here." She elbowed him in the ribs and slipped out from under his arm. His touch was too warm and she enjoyed it too much.

Dangerous feelings, a little voice in her head warned.

He shrugged. "Okay. Then I'll just say 'you're welcome.'"

She ignored the flash of hurt she'd seen in his expression when she moved away from him. "I'm sorry I can't pay you right away for all your work."

"No problem. I'm saving the money anyway." He stared at her, as if trying to see past her smile.

She concentrated on staying composed, trying to keep the mood light.

"Want to celebrate?" She wanted to feel like celebrating, even though she didn't. Maybe if they made a party of finishing up the house she would snap out of her glum mood.

His features relaxed. "Sure. What do you want to do? Dinner at The Victorian Inn?"

Oh, no. That would feel too much like a date. A romantic date. They were just friends. Hurriedly she said, "I was thinking more along the lines of dinner here. Maybe a bottle of wine." That was in keeping with her current budget, rather than an expensive dinner out.

Tony nodded in agreement. "Sure. Sounds good to me."

Keep it light, she told herself as they lapsed into silence. An easy dinner between friends, and then a quick goodbye.

There was no reason for Tony to spend the night tonight. The work was done.

Why did the thought make her feel like crying? Maybe she had PMS, she decided.

Move ahead, Julie. This is what you've been working for all summer. She looked down at her paint-smeared shirt and shorts. "I have to get cleaned up. I'm going to the real estate office and fill out the papers to officially list the place. I don't know how long that will take."

"While you do that I'll go get some groceries and take care of dinner."

She gave him a quick smile. "I was hoping you'd offer."

He laughed. "I figured."

Julie went up the freshly painted front steps, into the house and upstairs. She picked out a summer skirt and top, clean underwear and her sandals and carried everything into the bathroom.

While she showered and dressed she forced her thoughts away from Tony, refusing to dwell on missing him. Instead she planned the yard work and the inside cleanup she would do before the agent started showing the place.

Perhaps a hanging fern on the front porch and a few plants in the house to make it look more homey. There was still enough furniture to have it show well. If the new owners didn't want the antiques, Foggy Bottom would take them on consignment.

After she left for Los Angeles she would have to make sure the agent or someone else watered the yard and plants.

After she left.

She'd thought that being free to go back to L.A. would have lifted her spirits a little more.

Again she tried to shrug off the low mood. Tony would want to get back to working full time on his place. She thought of the tiny trailer and the Porta Potti and outdoor shower. He still had almost six weeks of warm weather left, but he needed to be in his house before the rain and cold weather set in.

That house was his dream. Just like writing was hers.

Separate dreams, separate cities.

Just the way it was supposed to be.

By the time she left the bathroom, Tony was gone and the house felt very empty.

Julie walked the two blocks to the real estate office. The agent was delighted to finally get the listing and told Julie he had a few buyers who might be interested. He was such a fast talking salesman she discounted his chatter and decided she would not count on potential buyers this soon, regardless of his boundless optimism.

They discussed the price of Victorians that had sold recently and compared them in size and condition to Julie's house.

She decided to set the selling price a little high to cover Tony's costs. She could always make counteroffers if she had to.

The whole process of listing the house with the real estate agent took much longer than she'd expected, and it was dark as she started for home.

She walked through the velvety warm summer night and stopped on the sidewalk out in front of the house. She looked at the structure with a critical eye, trying to feel what someone seeing it for the first time would feel.

It really was a charming old place, with its wide, wraparound front porch and graceful curves. The setting couldn't be more perfect, nestled among similar homes lining the quiet street.

Tony opened the front door, as if he'd been watching for her. No one had watched for her for a long time, and she liked the sensation of being welcomed.

"What are you doing out there in the dark?"

She laughed and started up the steps. "Trying to see it through the eyes of a prospective buyer."

He held the door open and motioned her in. "Come on in. It looks even better inside."

She followed him through the front door. Soft music played on her portable radio and the smell of grilled meat wafted in from the backyard. "Is that steak?" She asked, her mouth watering.

"Yeah. I brought my portable grill in yesterday."

She followed him into the kitchen and inhaled the wonderful scent. "Oh, it smells heavenly."

There was also a big green salad all ready to go on the counter and a loaf of sliced French bread in a basket.

He handed her a full glass of red wine, then picked one that was half-full up for himself. Gently he clinked his glass to hers. "In honor of the special occasion, a toast to finishing the house."

She nodded and took a sip of the excellent burgundy. "To finishing the house."

Then she brought her glass to his in another toast. "To you."

He looked startled. "Why?"

She touched her glass to his. "For not once saying I told you so."

He shook his head. "You could have done most of the fix-up yourself if you hadn't broken your collarbone."

She took another sip of wine. "You *are* an optimist. Want me to set the table?"

"It's done."

She glanced at the empty kitchen table.

"This is a celebration. We're eating in the newly refurbished dining room."

Julie turned and pushed the door open. Tony had set the table with cloth napkins and candles. There was a cut-glass vase of fresh flowers in the middle of the table.

A little fissure of warning cut through her. "It's beautiful." *And far too romantic.*

"Thanks. You bring in the salad and the bread and I'll grab the steaks."

Julie told herself to stay calm as she carried the wine and glasses to the table and then came back for the salad and bread. He hadn't planned the setting to be romantic, just to show off the room they had worked so hard to redo. She should leave the table set just like this. House hunters would be charmed.

Tony brought in two thick, sizzling porterhouse steaks and set them on the table, then came around and pulled out her chair. She felt a little jolt of panic at his polite, old-fashioned motion.

She chatted through dinner, determined to keep the mood light and friendly. She told him what the real estate agent had said about pricing the house and how quickly he thought it would sell.

Tony listened attentively and kept topping off her glass of wine. Because she was nervous, she kept sipping the wonderful burgundy.

By the time they finished the meal she felt all warm and flushed and thoroughly frazzled. She told herself she was being a fool for nothing. It was just a celebration between friends.

"That was terrific. Thank you." Julie stood up. "You cooked. I'll do the dishes."

He pulled the plate out of her hand and put it back on the table, then swung her into his arms. "The dishes can wait. I've never danced with you."

He spoke into the hair at her temple and a shivery thrill ran down her arms. He was a good dancer, she thought fuzzily as he maneuvered her through the double pocket doors into the living room where there was more floor space.

"I really need to do the dishes." She started to back out of his arms, and he held her in place.

"Why?" His breath nuzzled her temple.

She couldn't think of an answer and found herself wishing those clever lips of his would keep moving down until they got to her mouth.

Her arm crept up along his shoulder and her hand rested against his collar. She was warm and full and just a little tipsy from the wine. It felt so right to be there in his arms, dancing to the tinny sound of big band music coming through from the kitchen.

They made two circuits around the front room before the song ended. Julie tried to step back, but Tony didn't let go. She tipped her head back to give him a questioning look, and found his eyes fixed on her lips.

Her stomach did a funny little dip, and she raised up on her toes and brushed her lips across his.

His response was to cover her mouth with his and kiss her until her head was swimming and her body humming.

The next thing she knew they were on the couch and she was draped over his perfect body. He ran his clever hands from her shoulders to her thighs until she felt as if she would burst into flames.

"Julie." He groaned her name like a lament, then started back in on her mouth.

His hands slipped up under her skirt and caressed the backs of her knees until she thought she might weep with longing.

"Tony." Her voice was a breathy little whisper.

"What?" He groaned and hitched her higher, fitting her against him.

She moved her hips and felt his body respond. "Nothing. I just needed to say your name."

His hands went still on her thighs and she cursed herself for interrupting his upward journey. He reached up and peeled her hands away from his face, holding them between his palms. "We need to stop for a minute. I want to talk to you."

Julie didn't want to stop. She wanted him to keep on kissing her. She made a little sound of protest.

He brushed his mouth across her. "Hush. Listen to me."

With difficulty she focused on his face. "What?" Her voice sounded throaty and hoarse.

"We need to talk."

She didn't want to talk. She didn't want to think. "I need you to kiss me again." She leaned back toward his mouth.

Tony groaned and brought his hands up to her forearms, gently turning her, pushing her against the back of the couch.

"Julie, we're good together." He glanced down where her legs were still draped across his thighs.

No kidding, she thought, feeling like she was smoldering. She wanted him more than she'd ever wanted anyone. The thought sobered her up a little.

"I don't want to lose you. Stay here in Ferndale. We can work out where we'll live."

Suddenly the flush from the wine was gone. She knew what he was going to say and felt the panic start to build.

"I can't. I have to go back. I have a contract to teach."

"You still want to leave? You still want to live in L.A.?"

"No. Yes. I don't know. Why do you want me to stay?"

"Because I love you. I like it here, but if you can't live away from L.A., I'll go there."

She stared at him, openmouthed. "Don't say that!"

"I could survive in L.A."

"No, you couldn't. Besides, I wasn't talking about the city. I was talking about you saying you loved me. Don't say that."

He looked like she'd slapped him. "Why the hell not?"

Didn't he know how dangerous it was to fall in love?

How much he could get hurt? "Because I don't want you to."

His expression turned hard. "Well, tough. You don't get a say in it."

"What do you mean?" He said he was in love *with her*. Didn't that give her a right to comment?

He dropped his hands. "It's my feeling. I love you. You don't have to love me back, but don't tell me not to feel what I feel."

"You don't have to tell me you love me just to have sex. We can make love without all the declarations."

For an instant she saw violence in his face, a flash of the warrior he'd been. Then he visibly got a hold of himself and stood up so abruptly he almost dumped her off the couch.

"You think I told you I loved you to get you into bed." He was so angry he was vibrating with it.

She should take the words back, but she welcomed his anger. It was a safer thing to face than his declaration of love. "I've heard it before."

"Not from me you haven't."

"Tony, please, sit down." If she hadn't been in denial she would have seen this coming. She could have handled it better.

He refused to sit and stood glaring at her, so she stood up and faced him.

One of them had to be reasonable.

"I'm not going to love you. I don't love you." She lied. To him, and to herself. "I can't. I closed off that part of me after my parents died, and I'm not going there anymore. It hurts too much. If it didn't work out with us, I don't think I could survive it."

"What makes you think it wouldn't work out?" he ground out between clenched teeth.

Why couldn't he see? "It doesn't work out for couples

all the time. You think people fall in love thinking they'll fall out again? Or that one of them will find someone else?'' She hesitated for a long moment, and with a hitch in her voice continued, ''Or die? Everyone thinks it's forever. Well it's not. There aren't any guarantees.''

''Is that what you want? A guarantee? You'll close yourself off from being happy because there isn't any guarantee?''

He sounded disgusted, but Julie didn't care. He didn't know what the pain was like when you lost someone you loved. It had been more than ten years since her parents had been killed and the wound was still fresh. The bone-deep hurt never went away.

She felt the tears start, but she faced him anyway. ''You don't know what it's like.''

He reached for her and she stepped back.

She wiped at her wet cheek. ''I couldn't do that again. I couldn't.''

Tony gave a helpless little shrug. ''You want me to guarantee I'll outlive you. I can't do that. But I can promise I'll marry you and love you for the rest of my life.''

Julie gulped back a sob. ''That's not good enough.''

Tony looked heartbroken. ''Then I'm sorry. Because I can't promise you what you need to hear. Nobody can.''

Miserable, Julie swiped at her nose with the back of her hand. ''I know,'' she whispered.

''I'd better go.''

He turned and walked out the front door and down the steps. She watched him in the dim light from the porch as he climbed into his truck and pulled away.

She lay down on the couch that was still warm from his body and cried until she had no more tears.

Chapter Fourteen

It took Julie three days of backbreaking work to finish the yard and clean the house. She was determined to do it herself and exhaust herself in the process just so she could get some sleep.

It didn't work.

By the time she had pulled all the dead shrubs and cleared the weeds she was stuttering with fatigue, and she still wasn't sleeping at night.

Every time she heard a vehicle pass the house she would pause in her work, hoping it was Tony coming back.

Why couldn't she just let him go? she wondered. They couldn't resolve the breach between them. She couldn't, she amended to herself.

She was the problem.

Tony loved her, and that scared her half to death. Because in the middle of the night she lay awake in her bed and realized she loved him, too.

But she would not act on that love. She couldn't. She couldn't pay that price again.

She packed her car and dropped the house key off with the real estate agent.

She arrived back in L.A. in time for a killer heat wave and smog alert. She tried not to think about the clean, cool climate in Ferndale.

She moved her things back into her apartment and thought about going for a swim to cool off, then had a vision of Tony doing laps in the pool at her apartment.

Why had she brought him here? It would've been so much easier to move back if there were no memories of him in L.A.

Julie headed over to the high school to work in her classroom. Paula Johnston, who taught next door, stopped her on her way in.

"Good summer?" Paula's eyes narrowed as she took a good look at Julie. "Have you been sick? You look awful."

Trust Paula to leave the sugarcoating off. "No. Just tired. I just drove down from Northern California. Not used to the heat, I guess."

Paula looked as if she didn't believe a word Julie was saying, but she let it pass. "How long are you going to work?"

Until I feel like dropping, Julie wanted to say. "For a few hours. Why?"

"If we finish up at the same time, let's go grab dinner."

Both single, they often would go out on Friday nights when neither had a date. Julie didn't feel like going out, but she didn't want to be alone, either. "Okay. Check with me when you're almost done."

Julie unlocked her classroom door and stood staring at the bulletin boards that needed changing. She couldn't seem to summon the energy to do the project.

Paula came into her classroom two hours later. "Ready to knock off?"

Julie nodded and went for her purse. Might as well. She was getting nothing done here.

They drove separately and met at a popular restaurant several miles from school and settled into a booth.

Paula ordered a beer and Julie decided to stick with iced tea. "Did you hear about the enrollment?" Paula was a union representative and always had current information.

"No. I haven't seen anyone but you."

"Word is numbers are way down this year. We won't know until next week for sure, but some teachers may get reassigned."

Julie couldn't work up the energy to care, but she knew how important things like this were to Paula, so she listened and made appropriate comments.

Paula asked her again if she was okay. "You look like you've lost weight." She said it like it was an accusation.

"I worked all summer fixing up my grandmother's house to sell. I probably have." Actually she had eaten very little since the argument with Tony.

They chatted about school related things and then parted. Julie returned to her apartment and found a message on her machine. With a rush of hope she pushed the button to replay the message, hoping to hear Tony's voice. It was Steve, the real estate agent.

"I have two buyers interested in your place. I'll call you when the offers come in."

He'd only had the keys since yesterday morning. Julie figured it was a little optimistic to think there would be a buyer this soon and chalked it up to Steve's overconfidence.

She went to bed and had another restless night. She was aching, missing Tony, miserable.

About 2:00 a.m. Julie said the words out loud, testing them. "I love Tony."

At 4:00 a.m. she suspected that being without him hurt worse than losing him.

By the time the sun came up she wasn't sure she could survive without him.

Was she such a coward? Had she let the anger and unfairness of her parents' deaths fester for so long she had poisoned herself?

She was afraid the answer was yes.

Julie dragged herself out of bed and into the living room, to stare blindly at the TV news.

What was she going to do?

She dressed and returned to school. She could get a few hours of work in before the staff meeting started at nine. Heaven knows she hadn't accomplished anything yesterday.

As she worked she thought about her parents and realized she'd always blamed herself for their deaths, but she had blamed them, too. Double guilt. And at fourteen she'd had no one to talk her out of it.

She remembered her conversation with Tony about guilt. It was time to try to put the negative emotions away. She was no more responsible for her parents' death than they were. It had been a stupid, senseless accident.

Julie put her head down on her desk and cried until she fell asleep.

The next thing she knew, Paula was shaking her awake.

"Are you all right?" Paula looked alarmed.

Julie rubbed her eyes. "I'm okay. I was up most of the night clearing out some ghosts."

Paula drew up a chair. "Tell me."

Julie told her about her parents and the accident and going to live with Bessie.

"Oh, man. We both know how fragile kids are at that age. How did you survive?"

Julie shrugged. "Mostly by being angry and closing myself off. I didn't want to go back to Ferndale this summer because I thought I hated small towns, that one in particular. It isn't small towns. It isn't even Ferndale."

Paula made sympathetic noises and rubbed Julie's back.

It felt good to talk. "There's more. I made a decision a long time ago never to love anyone again because losing them hurt too much."

"That explains your dating habits. You've thrown guys away most women would give anything to have."

Julie started to cry again. "I think I threw away the one man I'd give anything to have."

"Who? Alan?" Paula sounded skeptical.

Julie laughed a watery laugh. She hadn't thought about Alan for months. "No. His name is Tony."

By the time Paula had pumped her for more information, it was time for the staff meeting.

Paula stood up. "Well, you have to make your own choices, but I think you'd be crazy to throw this thing away. Are you that much of a coward?"

Julie stared at her friend as she walked out of the classroom.

Julie paid little attention to the meeting. Her thoughts were too full of what Paula had said. Was she a coward?

On the drive back to her apartment her mind raced. Paula's words kept coming back to her. By keeping her heart locked away she could protect herself.

But at what cost?

She tried to imagine her life five years down the road. Would she be successful as a writer? And if she was, what else would she have? Would she spend her life writing books for other people's children and never having any of her own?

She let herself think about having children with Tony.

What would they look like? Would he be a good father? The answer to that question was yes. He was kind and considerate and would be a great role model for a child.

Her parents had died and left her behind. She had never looked at herself as their legacy, but she was. What would she leave behind?

Could she take the risk to find out?

When she got home there was a message from the real estate agent. He had two offers on her house and was meeting with a third couple this afternoon.

He called back around seven with two solid offers. They decided to go with the couple who had preapproved financing.

Julie hung up. She should be ecstatic. Instead she realized her one last tie to Ferndale was about to be severed.

She went to school the next day and met with her principal. She asked for a leave of absence and he was quick to say yes and lower the number of staff he had to juggle.

She collected her personal things from her classroom and left school. She should feel elated. Her dream to write was coming true.

She had no one to share the news with. The one person she wanted to tell was hundreds of miles away and didn't even have a telephone.

She went home feeling hollow and empty, yearning for something she had spent years convincing herself she didn't want.

If she went to see Tony, would he even talk to her? She had hurt him badly in her attempt to keep her heart locked away.

Suddenly she needed to find out. Needed to tell him she had made a terrible mistake.

Tony whacked at the dead limbs of the tree. The skeleton of the old oak was about fifty yards from the house and smack in the middle of his view of the Pacific Ocean. It would provide him with firewood for the whole winter. Fires he would sit in front of alone.

He didn't know what he was going to do when he finished with the tree. He'd hacked down everything in sight and still hadn't begun to work off the hurt Julie's leaving him had caused.

He paused to wipe the sweat off his forehead with the back of his gloved hand and heard the sound of a vehicle coming down his road.

He lifted his arm to shade his eyes against the glare of the late-afternoon sun and recognized Betty's Jeep.

What was Betty doing all the way out here? Tony wondered. He was in no mood for company. He hadn't showered today and bits of wood and bark stuck to the hair and sweat on his bare chest.

The vehicle disappeared behind his house and he heard the engine quit. Tony rested the ax beside the stump and walked to meet her.

Julie stepped out from the corner of the house and Tony's first thought was that his eyes were playing tricks on him.

She stood very still in the shadow of the west wall of his house.

What the hell was she doing here? The hurt rose up to choke him. He shoved it back down and stopped about ten feet from her.

"What do you want?" He saw her flinch at his rough tone.

"I wanted to bring you your money." She held out an envelope with the name of the real estate company in the return address corner.

The sight of her made his heart ache. Resolved to remember the pain her leaving had caused, he studied her for a full minute.

She looked thinner and pale. His quick assessment didn't miss the shadows under her eyes.

"You could have sent it."

She waved the envelope at him. "I...I wanted to give it to you. In person."

He noticed the way her hand shook. She held it out, waiting for him to take the money from her.

Tony's arms hung at his sides.

That envelope was the last link between them. If he took the money there would be nothing.

Foolish thought.

There was nothing now. She had killed that off when she had turned him down.

"Why? Why did you drive all the way out here?" He wasn't going to let her go so easily, not with the way he'd been hurting.

She lowered the envelope and looked past him, out toward the ocean. "I needed to apologize. For the way I left."

Tony didn't know what to say so he continued to stare at her.

She glanced at his face and then back out toward the water. "I lied to you."

He felt as if he couldn't breathe.

What had she lied about?

Was she married? Or engaged? He'd stayed at her place in Los Angeles. There'd been no sign of a man there. Separated? His mind ran wild over the possibilities and didn't find one that he wanted to accept.

"Lied about what?" he asked, his voice gruff with the anger he fought to control.

She sucked in a big gulp of air and started to cry. It was all he could do not to pull her into his arms and hold her.

"About loving you." she stuttered out the words on little sobs.

He took a step toward her, then stopped himself. That was not the only problem between them, but he felt a small glimmer of hope.

"What are you going to do about it?" If she was willing to commit to him despite her fears, he could meet her halfway.

He'd move to L.A.

He'd hate it, but it was better than not having Julie in his life.

She looked confused, and the silence stretched between them. "I'm not sure. What are you asking?"

He needed a commitment from her. A lifelong commitment. "My original offer still stands. Will you marry me?"

She looked terrified, but she nodded. "I'd like that. More than anything."

"Do you want me to move to L.A.?"

Julie looked surprised. "Would you do that? For me?"

Without hesitating he said, "Yes."

She started to cry again.

He stopped resisting the urge to touch her and covered the distance between them in two strides, enfolding her against his chest, wrapping his arms around her.

She was shaking and cold so he pulled her out of the shade and into the afternoon sunshine.

When her shaking subsided and her sobbing became little hiccups, he grasped her upper arms and pushed her gently away so he could see her face.

Her misery gave him the odd urge to smile. "Is that so awful? Loving me?"

She looked up at him with those big blue-green eyes he loved and in a shaking voice said, "I'm so scared."

He leaned in and kissed her on the forehead. "I know. And Julie-girl? I still can't give you any guarantees beyond loving you until I die."

"I know that. But I can't seem to get around the fact that I don't want to live without you. So I decided not to be afraid."

"How's that working for you?"

She laughed, a watery little sound. "Oh, some days are better than others."

"Do you think it would help if we tried it together? This 'not living without each other'?"

"Definitely." She slid her arms around his waist and buried her face against his chest.

He hugged her. "I smell like a mule."

She raised her head and licked his shoulder. "You smell wonderful."

His libido roared into overdrive and he has visions of hot sex right here on the ground next to his almost finished house.

He untangled her arms and knew if he didn't get some distance, they would get way ahead of themselves. There was still a great deal to be talked out here.

He let his eyes sweep over the land he loved. "Do we drive into town and put this place on the market?"

Julie shook her head, loving him all the more for offering. "No. I've been giving this a lot of thought. It isn't Ferndale in particular, or small towns in general I don't like." She needed to be absolutely truthful with him. "You were right. I was hiding in the city.

"In fact—" she stepped back and looked around "I think this might be a wonderful place to write. Not too many distractions."

He pulled her into his arms and brought his head down until their lips met. He dove into her mouth for a long kiss.

He looked pleased with the wanting look she gave him when he ended the kiss. ''After we get married I have a lot of distractions planned.''

She slid her arms around his waist and shoved her hands into the back waistband of his jeans, pulling him hard up against her. ''Oh, cowboy, I'm counting on that.''

*   *   *   *   *

Don't miss the latest miniseries from award-winning author Marie Ferrarella:

The **MOM SQUAD**

Meet...

Sherry Campbell—ambitious newswoman who makes headlines when a handsome billionaire arrives to sweep her off her feet...and shepherd her new son into the world!
A BILLIONAIRE AND A BABY, SE#1528, available March 2003

Joanna Prescott—Nine months after her visit to the sperm bank, her old love rescues her from a burning house—then delivers her baby....
A BACHELOR AND A BABY, SD#1503, available April 2003

Chris "C.J." Jones—FBI agent, expectant mother and always on the case. When the baby comes, will her irresistible partner be by her side?
THE BABY MISSION, IM#1220, available May 2003

Lori O'Neill—A forbidden attraction blows down this pregnant Lamaze teacher's tough-woman facade and makes her consider the love of a lifetime!
BEAUTY AND THE BABY, SR#1668, available June 2003

The Mom Squad—these single mothers-to-be are ready for labor...and true love!

Silhouette®
Where love comes alive™

DEBBIE

NEW YORK TIMES BESTSELLING AUTHOR

MACOMBER

*illuminates women's lives
with compassion, with love
and with grace. In* Changing Habits
*she proves once again why she's
one of the world's most popular writers
of fiction for—and about—women.*

*Changing
Habits*

---

*Available the first week of May 2003
wherever hardcovers are sold!*

MIRA®

COMING NEXT MONTH

#1666 PREGNANT BY THE BOSS!—Carol Grace

Champagne under the mistletoe had led to more than kisses for tycoon Joe Callaway and his assistant. Unwilling to settle for less than true love, Claudia Madison left him on reluctant feet. Could Joe win Claudia back in time to hear the pitter-patter of new ones?

#1667 BETROTHED TO THE PRINCE—Raye Morgan

Catching the Crown

Sometimes the beautiful princess needed to dump her never-met betrothed—at least that's what independent Tianna Roseanova-Krimorova thought. But a mystery baby, a mistaken identity and a surprisingly sexy prince soon made her wonder if fairy-tale endings weren't so bad after all!

#1668 BEAUTY AND THE BABY—Marie Ferrarella

The Mom Squad

Widowed, broke and pregnant, Lori O'Neill longed for a knight. And along came…*her brother-in-law?* Carson O'Neill had always done the right thing. But the sweet seductress made this Mr. Nice Guy think about being very, very naughty!

#1669 A GIFT FROM THE PAST—Carla Cassidy

Soulmates

Could Joshua McCane and his estranged wife ever agree on anything? But Claire needed his help, so he reluctantly offered his services. Soon, their desire for each other threatened to rage out of control. Was Joshua so sure their love was gone?

#1670 TUTORING TUCKER—Debrah Morris

The headline: "West Texas Oil Field Foreman Brandon Tucker Wins $50 Million, Hires Saucy, Sexy Trust Fund Socialite To Teach Him The Finer Things In Life." The *Finer Things* course study: candlelight kisses, slow, sensual waltzes, velvety soft caresses…

#1671 OOPS…WE'RE MARRIED?—SUSAN LUTE

When career-driven Eleanor Rose wanted to help charity, she wrote a check. She did *not* marry a man who wanted a mother for his son and a comfortable wife for himself. She did *not* become Suzy Homemaker…*nor* give in to seductive glances… or passionate kisses…or fall in love. Or did she?

SRCNM0503